MYTHOS

A Novel

By Jaysen Headley

Mythos

A Novel by Jaysen Headley

Cover Art by Jonathan Perry

Senior Editor: Carl Ka-Ho Li

© 2019 by Jaysen Headley

© 2019 Cover Art by Jonathan Perry

ISBN 978-0-9908283-4-1

This book is printed in the United States of America

For LaQuita,

For your kindness, your humor, and for believing in this book from day one.

Ever since Dawson Saks first stood up on live TV three years ago and announced the official opening of Mythos— a zoo for magical creatures—I thought of nothing but getting my foot in the front gates. My dreams were consumed by visions of flying on dragon-back, riding a unicorn and swimming with kelpies. Now, as I sit in the lounge assigned to Class B, on the second floor of a cruise ship bound for the little island off the coast of the Florida peninsula which Mythos calls home, I wish I could be anywhere but here.

"You're staring," says Erika, one of my best friends. I guess I should say my only best friend now. My only friend at all, really. Erika, Zach and I all met on our first day of first grade. And now here we are together at the ripe old age of sixteen, and for the first time ever Zach isn't hanging out with us, which is my fault. "It's not your fault," she says. Lies! "He'll come around."

A couple months ago, when our school submitted the forms to enter to win a free trip to the park, I made a bet with the Universe. I told the Universe that if we got the chance to go on this trip and actually won, I'd come clean and stop lying to all my friends and family. Then, the unthinkable happened. We won. We actually won. And it's not like you can just back out of a bet with the Universe. That's bad form. So, I stopped lying and came out to my family and to my friends. My dad seemed alright, which was fairly surprising considering most Chinese parents I know wouldn't be. Then again, my dad's always been the most progressive member of his super conservative family. Case in point, he was the first of them to move to the U.S. back in the 80's. But my mom was furious. She swore in Mandarin and then proceeded to give me the silent treatment, which is how I know when she's really mad. In fact, since I told her, she hasn't spoken English once, which sucks because I was born in Connecticut and my Mandarin is atrocious.   Erika took it pretty well. She said she always kind of figured, but Zach freaked out. His family is pretty conservative, so I guess he's having a hard time processing, and while I want to give him space, I can't help but feel pretty pissed off at him. I mean, he's my friend. He's supposed to be there for me. But no. He can't do that because he was raised to think that every gay man wants to get in his pants and force him to sin. Not to say that I haven't thought about it once or twice, but at the

2

end of the day he's like a brother to me, and that would just be weird.

Zach is pretty good looking though. He's got this medium length hazel hair that swoops and curls in all the right places like Clark Kent, which probably means he does nothing to it in the morning—just showers and goes—and that's infuriating, considering how hard I have to try to get my thick black hair to look naturally messy. Every morning I try for an hour and a half to look like I didn't try at all.

"You're fixating," says Erika, shaking my shoulder. She has dark skin and even darker hair which she's shaped into ribbon-like curls with fashionable blond highlights striped throughout. And she has these big beautiful brown eyes that always remind me of how gay I am because if I were even a little straight, I'd fall for her just by looking into those eyes. She always smells like strawberries, and she always wears the cutest outfits and god, one day, she's going to help shape the world. She already has more Instagram followers than everyone else in our class combined. She's the queen of the perfect selfie. I hate her for that. But she's got a big heart and an even bigger brain. I love her for that.

"I'm not. You are!" I say in a totally mature sort of way. I sigh heavily and dramatically. I'm pretty good at being dramatic. "I just want to get through the part where we aren't talking and get to the part where he straight-guy fist bumps me and is like 'okay so you like dudes, whatever.' Can't we just be there already?"

"It will come," laughs Erika. "But you told us two weeks ago. The wound is still fresh."

"Me being gay is not a wound."

"You know what I mean." Mid-pout, she pulls out her phone and takes a quick selfie that I'm half in.

"Please don't tag me in that," I say. "I look horrible."

"You always look perfect, Henry."

I groan as I lean over and look out the panoramic window that's just behind the navy-blue loveseat we're sitting in. The whole lounge is done in a nautical theme with anchors and oars hanging from the walls and ceiling. I get the overwhelming impression that we're inside either the cleanest lighthouse ever or the perfect summer ad from a Pottery Barn magazine.

The ocean outside is racing by under a cloudless sky. I still can't believe I'm about to go to this amazing place I've read everything about and even dreamed about, and here I am feeling miserable. Life sucks. Hoping to feel better, I try to picture the park, or rather what I remember from TV and all the Mythos blogs. I close my eyes and picture the huge gray stone of the Grand Palace, a castle which stands as a centerpiece to the park's main guest area, with its high towers topped with regal flags waving gallantly in the wind. It, along with several shops, restaurants and attractions, sits at the southern end of the park in a centralized hub, known adorably as Town Square. The castle is mostly a facade for the visitor center and a huge gift shop where you can buy mythical creature merch. I, for one, have my heart set on a cockatrice plushie I've been eying on the Shop Mythos website. They also do a big fireworks show over the castle at night. Think the Magic Kingdom in Orlando but bigger.

But obviously the part I'm most excited for is not the fireworks or the merch. I mean, I'm pretty excited for the merch, but no. The most exciting part of going to a park full of mythical creatures is the mythical creatures themselves. The park's been open for about a year-and-a-half now, and people the world over are still in awe at how this guy, Dawson Saks, managed to genetically engineer everything from dragons to unicorns to fairies. No one really knows how he did it either. It's sort of the best-kept secret outside of Arby's special sauce. All sorts of scientists have tried to figure it out. Reporters have tried to coax it out of Saks in interviews, but no luck. The guy gets real cagey. He might have been a politician in a past life because I don't know if I've never seen someone dodge a question with such finesse. "Why magic, of course," he always says when asked how he's done it in interviews. "What else?" At this point, it's practically his tagline.

All I know is, this guy knows something the world can't figure out, and that makes me a little bit obsessed with him. After all, how many secrets are really left in the world nowadays thanks to the internet?

"Think I should say hi to the new guy?" asks Erika, jostling me from my daydreams. I turn from the window to look over at the new guy in question.

Noah Henson. No relation to Jim Henson or at least I don't think there is. He just transferred to our school a couple months back, but with all the excitement of going on this trip, no one has really taken the time to get to know him. He's sitting, lounging really, with his earbuds in, staring at his phone, in a navy armchair on the opposite end of the lounge underneath a huge antique, wooden ship steering wheel. He's totally managed to block out the group of three cackling girls and another set of guys laughing so hard that snot is coming out of their noses. Super attractive guys. Really.

Noah looks like the kind of guy who doesn't want to be bothered, like, ever. He's wearing this dark green shirt and a metal grey beanie, which he always wears so that the top hangs off the back of his head. Think Link from The

Legend of Zelda but more subtle. He's got on black jeans with holes in the knees and black converse, which are totally classic. He always dresses a bit emo in an organic, not Hot Topic, kind of way. The thing I always notice about him though is his eyes which are so green you'd think they were emeralds. They look a little fake, to be honest. Like, maybe he wears colored contacts.

"I just feel bad," says Erika. And she probably does. A lot of people have this fake way of wanting to get to know the 'new kid' or 'the kid that everyone picks on' in order to somehow feel better about how shitty they are the other 99% of the time; but Erika isn't like that. She has this amazing empathic connection to the world, which is just a fancy way to say that she's actually a good person who cares about people in a non-selfish way. I wish I could do that. I'm fairly self-centered. I know that. Chalk it up to being an only child or whatever, but I often realize that I'm only thinking about myself, or worse, only talking about myself. Then I have to physically force myself to see things from another person's perspective or just stop talking. The fact that not being self-obsessed is so hard for me is something I hate about myself.

"I don't think you need to feel bad," I say. "He looks pretty content. I mean, if you wanted someone to talk to you, would you leave your headphones in and not talk to anyone?"

"Maybe he's shy?"

And then it hits me. "Oh my God. You think he's cute!"

"Stop!" She tries to shut me up by actually putting her hand over my mouth, like he might hear me from the other side of the room through whatever most-likely-grunge-emo-pop song he's listening to.

"You do!" I insist, pushing her back.

"Don't you think he is?" she asks hesitantly, almost surprised by the very notion of her question.

I go to answer, but it seems to hit both of us that this is the first time we have ever talked about boys like this. It's the first time we're openly acknowledging that we play for the same team: the boy-crazed team.

"Well . . ." I start, not entirely sure how this is supposed to work. I mean, I learned most of what I know about being gay by watching old reruns of Will and Grace on Hulu, but I'm no Will Truman and she is certainly no Grace Adler so where does that leave us? "I guess . . ." I say, trying to keep it casual, even though now I'm blushing because I'm staring at Noah and thinking about him like that.

Then, of course, he looks up and sees me staring like a moron. I look away as fast as I can, but I'm sure he saw me and now I'm even redder.

"You guess?" Erika asks. She's been looking at me this whole time and didn't see the awkward bomb that just exploded. "Have you even seen his eyes? That boy has movie star eyes."

"Yeah, sure," I say, taking in the fine architecture of the ceiling because where else do I even look at this point? I think I might just spend the rest of my life looking up, so I never have to endure making eye contact with a cute boy ever again.

Suddenly I hear a laugh I recognize and realize that it's Zach laughing with these two other guys. I can't help but think that he's laughing loudly to try and force the illusion that he's happier without us. It's insufferable.

"Ugh."

"It's cool," says Erika, who apparently also heard the laughter. "This too shall pass Henry Lau."

"Don't use my full name like you're my mother." But I laugh because I like it when Erika acts like my mom. She's definitely the more mature one of the two of us, which is good because I need a guide through the maze of life that is being a teenager. She's like my sherpa through the mountains of adolescent anxiety.

"So, what do you want to do first when we get there?" she asks me, pulling out her phone and opening up the official Mythos app. It has things like wait times, show times, where to find food, and the nearest restroom. It also has a game you can play in the park where you discover virtual versions of the mythical creatures and become friends with them.

"Well, we won't go on the big park tour until tomorrow," I say with disappointment. "So, we should use today to check out the Town Square and the visitor's center, look at merch and definitely try the dragon waffles, unicorn shakes, and medieval cookie sandwiches." I pause here to let her know how important this is. "It's a cookie sandwich inside of another cookie sandwich."

"You and your desserts," she laughs. "Do you have to know what desserts are available everywhere you go?"

"What do I look like to you? Some kind of monster?" I give her an overdramatic sideways grin, as if to answer my own rhetorical question with a resounding "yes!"

"Yes," she says. "You cookie monster."

I love sweets, especially cookies, which will probably catch up with me someday in the form of a large belly, but for now I'm pretty slim and don't really gain weight, and I intend to take full advantage of it while I can.

"Oh! We can also go to the Kraken Amphitheater and watch them feed the Kraken," I say, realizing that the Kraken Amphitheater is within walking distance from the visitor center, which is next door to The Blue Loch, the hotel we'll be staying at. There are three hotels and it's the more economical of the three, if anything on the island can be labeled as such. There's a mid-range cost hotel, The Ethereal Odin, and then there's the VIP hotel, The Fownchimer, which is the most luxurious and expensive. Let me be very clear here; even the cheapest hotel in Mythos is still worlds classier and more expensive than any other hotel on Earth. Universal Studios and Disney World have the benefit of being on the mainland where guests can stay in off-site hotels that are lower on cost, but because Mythos was built on an island owned by Dawson Saks, there aren't any other options. You either pay to stay or you stay nowhere, which isn't an option. In any other circumstance, I'd by lucky to enter the lobby of one of these resorts, let alone sleep in one of their beds.

Erika looks up and bites the inside of her cheek, which she always does when she's thinking about something. "I'm going to invite new kid to hang with us," she says, as if she's making a New Year's resolution.

"Seriously?" I honestly can't decide if the idea of hanging out with Noah the green-eyed monster is a good idea or a bad one.

She promptly stands up and crosses the room towards him. I follow along like a kid following his Mom into a lotion store. Like, I don't really want to go with her, but what choice do I honestly have here? We walk through the room filled with chatting teens, and I can't help but look to see if Zach is watching us. He's not. I look away before he notices me. I can't deal with unwanted eye contact twice in one day.

I don't really know why eye contact stresses me out so much. Maybe I feel like that person can see into my soul, past all the bullshit that I'm projecting into the world as a way of shielding myself. Whatever the case may be, people who step to the side to meet my gaze after I've clearly looked away are my nemesis. Teachers, in particular, are frequent offenders to this personal rule.

"Hey," says Erika as we reach Noah. He continues to stare at his phone screen, oblivious to our presence.

Erika clears her throat and then says, louder than before, "Hey!"

Noah looks up and it's like we've pulled him out of some sort of trance. He seems confused like he has no idea where he is or how he got here. His green eyes dart around the room and then back to us. I have to steady myself because, as corny as it sounds, I feel like I might just fall into them. He removes his earbuds and just stares at us for a long moment. Long enough that I realize I've forgotten to breathe.

"Sup?" he asks. I instantly feel a little deflated because I realize in that moment that he's not gay. Or at least I don't think he is. Do gay guys say 'sup?' I don't really know. I don't say it, that's for sure. I know there's this whole idea of gaydar, and I don't know if the ability is specific to those who are gay or not, but I guess I haven't developed that powerset yet. Maybe as I get more in touch with what it means to be gay, I'll start to feel a tingling sensation like the awakening of a mutant power? I mean, statistically speaking, SOMEONE else in my class or my school should be gay, but so far, if there is, they're staying pretty tight lipped about it. And now I'm looking at Noah's lips, which is better than staring into his forest-like eyes, I guess?

"We're gonna check out the gift shop after we drop off our stuff at our hotel and then watch the Kraken eat a jeep." She ponders this for a brief moment. "Or whatever they eat." She shakes her head and smiles. "Anyway," she refocuses herself, "wanna hang out with us?" She's super chill. Super casual. I'm both impressed and jealous that she's so good at talking to strangers. It comes so natural to her.

Noah looks from Erika to me and then back to Erika. Then, as if we never even walked all the way over here, he puts his earbuds back in, leans back into his chair, and goes back to staring at his phone screen. "I'm good," he says as an afterthought.

Erika's head jerks back and her face visibly contorts into an expression of disgust. "Um, rude much?"

I look down in embarrassment at my red pumas and turquoise shorts that are rolled up, revealing my bony knees. The sight of them consumes me with a sudden wave of self-consciousness. I'm wearing a white and black striped t-shirt, which I'm now worried makes me look like a prisoner in an old black and white movie. I was much more confident getting dressed this morning when I viewed myself in the mirror and was sure the look worked. Now, all of that has been replaced with self-doubt. It's a rare day in hell that I feel confident in my own skin, and today is not shaping up to be one.

"Erika, let's just go," I say to her under my breath, pulling on her arm.

"No," says Erika, snapping me out of my self-hate spiral. "We aren't going to just go. I'm being nice here." She glares at Noah, who looks up again, pulling out one ear bud. "We could've just left you over here to stew by your lonely self, but we decided to extend a hand of friendship, you big jerk!"

"I'm not lonely," snaps Noah. "And I don't need your charity or your pity. So, like I said," he annunciates his next words like we're watching Sesame Street and he's teaching us to say the word of the day. "I'm. Good."

He puts the earbud back in his ear and goes back to his phone. Erika's face contorts as rage overcomes her, but whatever vicious retort she's concocting gets sidelined when Mr. Zeckel, Class B's homeroom teacher, enters the room. He's wearing a Hawaiian shirt, khaki shorts and flip flops, all topped off with a wide brimmed straw hat. He claps his hands three times in a rhythm he's programmed us to respond to. We all echo the clap in response, then give him our undivided attention.

"Alright explorers," he starts, because somewhere in his head we're all five-year-olds and not sixteen and seventeen. The 'explorers' comment gets more than a couple eye rolls. "We are about to dock so everyone should head back to their rooms and grab their belongings. Who's excited?!"

There are a few claps and cheers. I mean, yeah, despite our overly enthusiastic teacher acting like the host of Blue's Clues, we're all fairly excited to get to see a real-life dragon.

"Um, I'm sorry," he says putting a hand to his ear. "I don't think I heard you. Let's try that again. I said, who's excited?"

This time everyone cheers louder, hoping that if we

yell loud enough, he'll leave us the hell alone. "Better," says Mr. Zeckel.

As a collective mass of student cattle, we all head for the double doors at the end of the lounge which will take us to the elevators that descend down into the ship and back to our respective cabins on the lowest passenger level. If this were the Titanic, we'd be denied lifeboats for sure.

I can't even explain why I do it, but before I walk through the doors, I look back at Noah. I guess maybe I want to see if even the event of getting to Mythos is enough to get anything more than a smug look on his face. But to my surprise, he's no longer staring at his phone screen.

Instead, his eyes are fixed on me. Me. He's staring right. At. Me. Holy shit. His eyes are so green. I can't even deal. And I want to look away. I need to look away, but it's like I'm being hypnotized.

"Oh my god Henry, stop staring!" says Erika. She grabs my hand and sarcastically says, "Okay now, let's all hold hands so we don't get lost." I break my line of sight with Noah as she pulls me into the crowd. "What a jerk, right?" she's still upset by Noah's response to her as we board the elevator, packed in like sardines. Thomas Ruiz, this goofy kid in my class is practicing his best 'scary face,'

16

for some girls and keeps bursting into these horrified looks that you usually only see from damsels in horror movies.

"And this is what I'm gonna look like when I see the bunyip," he says right before his face squinches up so that he looks like that evil girl from The Ring. I have to admit, it's pretty funny, but the laughter is shaking the elevator and after my brief bout with seasickness yesterday when we first set out to sea, I'm seriously hoping I don't have a return trip to Pukesville.

At last, the doors open to my floor. I squeeze through the group and wave bye to Erika. My room is third on the left and I'm sharing it with Zach, who isn't talking to me so that's awesome. When we chose roommates, I was still 'totally-into-girls Henry,' as opposed to my new status quo, 'gayer-than-the-day-is-long Henry.'

I take a deep breath before entering, mentally preparing for the awkward silence that hangs like the thick Florida summer air whenever we're within three feet of each other. But to my surprise, he's already come and gone, taking his luggage with him. I sigh in relief and grab my rolling red suitcase and messenger bag before leaving the cabin behind. I take one more selfie on my phone and post it to Instagram with the caption: 'And so it begins.' Then it's back down the elevator, which is still crowded, but this time with all sorts of people and their luggage jammed into every square inch of space between our legs and me shoved against the pinstripe-wallpapered walls.

I emerge back into the lounge and wait around for a while until Erika finally appears. She has two rolling suitcases and two more smaller bags, one slung over each shoulder.

"I still don't understand why you have to bring so much stuff," I say.

"Because," she says, letting the two smaller bags fall to the floor beside us with a heavy thud. "It takes a lot of stuff to make this happen every day. She waves her hands to indicate her cute outfit and flawless makeup as she smiles and tilts her head to the side in a perfect cute-anime-girl pose.

"If you say so," I laugh.

The boat docks and after a little more downtime while the ship's crew gets everything secured, we follow the line of passengers down a ramp, getting our first view of the massive island which looks like a tropical paradise full of thick jungles, scenic waterfalls, white sandy beaches, and majestic mountains just waiting to be explored. And dammit if that thought doesn't make me cringe when I'm reminded of Mr. Zeckel's explorer comment.

As we step onto the dock, I can feel everyone's excitement crackling through the air as we catch our first glimpse of the Mythos sign next to the train station where the train that will take us to our hotel and the main hub of the park awaits. It looms over us like a challenge to leave the world we know behind for anyone who dares to pass beneath it.

"Welcome to Mythos" it says in swooping gold font against a black background. And in smaller letters on a second line: "Believe Everything." I am awestruck. And for the first time it really hits me.

I'm here.

I probably sound a little boy crazy at this point. But come on, I just came out. I'm sixteen (seventeen next month), and if boys weren't the only thing I thought about before I came out, they certainly are now. I guess when you come out to your friends and family, you also have to come out to yourself. Like, you finally decide that all your questions about your sexuality finally need to get the hell out of your life. You decide to be yourself, and no longer care who knows. You try, anyway.

I know I was just ogling Noah. Jerk face, rude AF Noah. But I'm sitting on the Comet, the Mythos sky-train that transports guests from the pier to the Town Square and all the adjoining resorts and guest areas, when I see this guy sitting a few seats down across from us. This in itself wouldn't be a big deal except that he's smiling and making bedroom eyes at me. At least I assume they're bedroom eyes. I know I would for sure love it if some guy made those eyes at me in my bedroom. Crap, now I'm blushing.

I should probably explain that maybe due to the fact that until a couple weeks ago, I wasn't out, or maybe because I'm this short Chinese kid who's socially awkward and prefers to read or research the financial structure of Mythos, I don't really get a lot of male attention. Did I say a lot? I meant I get NO male attention. It's not like I know a lot of gay guys in the first place. And my one attempt at trying to go to a gay bar ended in me getting turned away for being too young. I know everyone my age has a fake ID, but I'm sort of a rule follower and can't bring myself to get one.

But now, here I am sitting on these cushioned seats which line the car's outer walls and this boy is staring at me and smiling. He looks kind of shy about it, but not shy enough to look away. It doesn't help that he's my ideal type of guy in the looks department. He's like half Nick Jonas, half Jesse McCartney and half Shawn Mendes. Okay, maybe that is too many halves, but contrary to stereotypes, I suck at math. Even my teachers have tried to get me to tutor other kids on the assumption that I was somehow born an algebra god. Sorry, Mrs. Fink, I suck at algebra and trig, and even simple equations give me a run for my money. Oh, and PS, that's discrimination.

But back to this guy. Did I mention he's gorgeous? Wavy jet-black hair, glistening blue eyes, dimples and freckles perfectly placed on his face. If I didn't know better, I'd say he was manufactured in the same facility where they make Ken dolls. He's wearing this loose long-sleeved white shirt which looks semi-transparent and tight black jeans with black flip-flops hanging lazily from his toes. His skin is pale and reminds me of a smooth undisturbed beach in Vero where my parents took us on vacation last summer. The really weird thing is that although everyone in this train car is from our class, I can't remember ever seeing him before.

"Hey," I say, nudging Erika, who's sitting next to me editing a photo on her phone to post later. I can already see the 'likes' flooding in and the comments declaring her 'Goddess' or 'Queen.'

"Hm?" she glances over at me absently as she types out her caption.

"Do you know who that guy is?" I casually motion with my eyes to where he's sitting.

She looks up for a second and then back down, and I love her a little bit more than usual because of how sly and unobvious she is. Like she instinctively knows that we are checking out a guy, which is serious business. Subtlety is key.

"Nope," she says. "Maybe he's one of the band kids?"

Class B technically won the free trip to Mythos. You already know that part. But we didn't do it all on our own. The contest was to create a commercial for the park. Class B just so happened to be comprised of mostly theater, band and other arts-minded kids. So, we ended up banding together and using all our acting, crafting and musical skills to create this epic commercial for the park that I swear actually made a few parents cry when we showed it to them in an after-school screening. There were big cut outs of dragons and Janice Makfen even brought in her pony which we strapped a horn from our props department to so that it looked like a unicorn. Janice's whole family is pretty loaded, in case that wasn't obvious. The only thing we outsourced from the Class B students was music because, well, you need more than a couple kids to make an epic soundtrack to an epic commercial. So, we pulled in some band kids and put together this soaring soundtrack that's like *Game of Thrones* meets *Jurassic Park*. And of course, anyone who helped with the commercial got to go to the park, which meant the band kids that volunteered got to join Class B on the trip.

And in answer to your question as to what my talent is: I play the cello. My mother gave me three choices when I started elementary school: cello, flute or death. She swears that cello and flute are the most likely instruments to get a scholarship with. I swear she made that statistic up. In any case, I chose the lesser of three evils. I actually like playing the cello but hate carrying the thing to and from school every day. I'm in orchestra and know most of the band kids, but marching band has a few people who *only* do marching band. So, Erika is right: he totally could be in marching band.

He looks around himself for a moment and then stands and walks towards me. TOWARDS ME! I'm freaking out because what do I even say to this boy that won't sound completely stupid? How do you even talk to someone this gorgeous? I'm not emotionally prepared for this. There's this little bit of space on the seat next to me between myself and Thomas Ruiz, who's currently explaining to the girl on his other side why his family thinks Mythos is bad for the world economy. I get the feeling he's just trying to impress her, and it's working. She's looking at him like he's the smartest kid in our class. His voice fades into the background as blue-eyes sits down next to me, squeezing into the small space so that our thighs are up against each other.

I feel like there's an alien in my chest ready to burst out, but then I realize it's just my heart. What is happening? I don't even know. I try to speak but end up breathing like the singers in our class when they're warming up their vocal chords—heavy, thick, unattractive breaths. It's like the first time I listened to *Dear Evan Hanson*. Or the first time I saw *Rent* and the cast performed "Seasons of Love." If this were a cartoon, my whole body would melt into goo and I'd just drip off the seat onto the floor. Some janitor would come in after hours to mop me into a bucket. But it's not a cartoon, so I try to smile back with . . . mixed results.

"Hey, I'm Erika," says Erika, reaching over my speechless self with her extended hand.

"Vincent," he says, shaking her hand. I notice a bulky silver ring on his middle finger. I've apparently become invisible, which at this point is a good thing because I can't form words or thoughts anyway.

"You're one of the band kids, right?" she asks.

He seems confused at first, but then smiles at her and nods. "Totally. How'd you know?"

"I'm psychic," she says with a little wink.

"She really is," I blurt out. Am I yelling? It sounds like a might be yelling. "She totally knew I was gay before even I did." What? What did I just say? Did I just come out to this total stranger? Why are my hands sweating so much? Have my cheeks always felt this hot?

To my enormous surprise, Vincent laughs. "You're cute," he says through his laughter—his perfect, adorable laughter. My whole body freezes, like I'm being held in place by some invisible force. But it's really just my nerves because no one has ever called me cute before. Okay, my Mom probably has, and my weird aunt does at Christmas, but this is totally different. This is an unsolicited compliment by a beautiful guy.

"This is Henry," says Erika, coming to my rescue. "We're going to check out the gift shop and watch the Kraken show after we drop off our bags at the resort. You wanna join us?" she asks like it's the easiest thing in the world. Like talking to cute guys isn't the most stressful part of waking up each and every day.

"Sure," he says, like saying yes to hanging out with new people isn't the most stressful part of waking up each and every day. Yes, everything is stressful every morning. Is that not normal? "I'd love to." And then he winks at me. What the *what*?! Is this real life? Or maybe I'm just dreaming? Maybe I dozed off during *Riverdale* and now I'm dreaming about cute guys winking at me and calling me cute. But this must be real life because what kind of monster would I be if I fell asleep during *Riverdale*?!

I don't have time to process any of this because the train comes to a stop and an announcer's voice comes through the speakers above us: "Welcome to Mythos Town Square. All guest resorts. The Grand Palace and the

Kraken Amphitheater. Please wait until the train comes to a complete stop before moving about the cabin."

Much like my school trip to New York City when I was in Middle School, no one waits for the train to stop. They all get up and cling together at the sliding double doors. Erika stands and grabs both of our shoulder bags down from the overhead compartment, handing mine to me. The rest of our bags will be transported to the hotel and be waiting for us when we arrive. I take it and turn to look for Vincent, but he's disappeared into the crowd, and even though the train car isn't that big, I've somehow managed to lose him entirely to the throngs of people excited to disembark and finally get their vacations underway.

"I am like the best wing-woman ever," says Erika proudly. "All other wingers should bow before me and bask in my glory."

"What are you talking about?" I roll my eyes. "And what's a winger?"

"I just totally got you a date," she says.

"Is it a date if it will be all three of us?"

"You don't even know that guy," she cuts back. "Trust me, if it goes south, you'll be happy to have me as your exit strategy. And if it goes well . . ." she fake coughs into her hand. "I think I might have eaten some bad shellfish on the ship." She winks at me. Why is everyone so winky today? It's freaking me out. "Just admit it. I'm awesome."

I sigh. "At least you were able to talk to him. I think my voice freaked out and went to recess."

"You're an embarrassment to your people," she says.

"The Chinese?" I'm confused.

"The gays," she snaps. "Sooner or later you're going to have to learn how to flirt *without* my help."

"Nope," I say. "You'll be with me to talk to guys forever and ever." I smile hopefully.

She scoffs as the double doors to the train open and we follow the crowd out.

Truth is, there was a time where I thought both she *and* Zach would be around forever, but with things the way they are with Zach now, everything is much less certain.

The three of us met in first grade when Zach pushed Erika because, as you may have heard, girls are icky. Erika fell backwards into me and suddenly I was part of the whole mess. We all got sent to time out. Over time, we went from hating each other to discussing what kind of bender we would be if we were on *Avatar: The Last Airbender* to finally doing one of those pacts of friendship where we spit into our hands and shook on it. A binding seal of friendship if ever there was one. But maybe there was something magical in the spit that day, because it stuck. Erika and Zach were there for my first B on my report card (an F in my household). Zach and I were there for Erika's first crush on a boy (Michael B. Jordan). She still claims their love affair is written in the stars. And we were there for Zach's first broken arm, followed by a broken leg. And then another broken arm. Zach loves sports and outdoor activities. I vividly remember his mother gasping in horror at the first bone break and rolling her eyes as if bored by the fourth. All of these memories play out in my head to a mixture of sentiment and regret as we step off the train.

Outside, the sun is beaming down on us and the air is sticky and hot. There's no doubt that we're in a tropical paradise. From the train platform, we can see all the way down the center of the Town Square. Shops, and restaurants line either side of a wide cobblestone street which ends with an enormous, multi-towered castle at the opposite end. The resorts are actually located behind the castle to either side, but we can't see them from here due to the storefront facades that obscure our view past them. The whole thing takes my breath away. It's like the first time my family ever visited Disney World except elevated to a whole new level. The stores and castle are bigger. The music is more joyous. And the knowledge that the creatures we'll find here are real and not simply animatronics is enough to set Mythos in a league of its own.

All the colors along the street are vibrant and rich with storefronts calling out to us in bold magentas, forest greens and electric blues. Musicians playing instruments from medieval times walk the street wearing costumes straight out of *Spamalot,* one of my favorite musicals. It's based on *Monty Python and the Holy Grail,* so you know it's amazing. The sounds of bagpipes, pan flutes and lutes fill the air in a cacophony that seems to draw us forward. The smell in the air is a combination of fragrant breads, roasting turkey, salted creams, and—my mouth waters at the thought—fresh from the oven cookies.

"Erika. I smell cookies!"

"All of this," she motions to the view before us, "and your first thought is cookies?"

"Always," I say. But she's right. There is so much to see and smell and hear. I feel like my senses are being bombarded from every direction. But nothing compares to the majestic sight of the castle at the far end of the Square. In my head I know the Grand Palace, as it's called, is just a gift shop. Well, it's not JUST a gift shop. The first floor has a gift shop and guest relations. The second floor is a five-star restaurant and the rest of the floors above that are

Mythos Central Command where the park is run via engineers and technicians. The point is, I know that, but looking at it, all of that falls away and I feel as though I've been transported to some mythical place out of time and space. Like maybe I'm actually walking down a street in some fantasy medieval European town, and any moment now, a werewolf will attack or perhaps a dragon will swoop down and breathe fire.

"I can't believe we're actually here," I say, mostly to myself, but loud enough that Erika hears me.

"Yeah, it's pretty breathtaking," she says. "Genevieve, you know the one who's a year under us on the track team with me, came here with her Dad when they first opened, and she said she broke down in tears the first time she saw Town Square. I thought she was full of shit, but . . ." She reaches up and wipes her eyes. "Guess I was wrong."

She's right. It's pretty amazing that we're here. When you see it on the news or read about it, no matter how much you imagine being here, it's still so distant. And even when you see dragons and unicorns in pictures or on YouTube, it's hard to be too affected by it, considering we grew up with *Game of Thrones* and virtual reality video games where anything is possible. But now that we're standing here, the reality of it seems to wash over both of us. My skin tingles like I'm being hit with a wave of actual real-life magic.

I smile and wrap my arm around her, keeping my eyes out for Vincent. I can't quite explain it, but ever since our eyes locked on the train, I can't seem to get the thought of him out of my mind. Maybe this is what everyone talks about when they say "love at first sight." I also purposefully avoid looking for Zach because seeing him scowling at me might just be the only thing that could ruin this moment and I'd like to avoid his judgy eyes as much as possible.

"Come on," I say. We head down the main street which looks like it's made of thick cobblestones, but it's actually an optical illusion, which means you get the aesthetic of cobblestones without the bumpy path.

We pass by a cart selling Unicorn Popcorn, which we obviously buy to try because it's basically popcorn with cotton candy flavored sprinkles on top so that it looks like a glitter bomb exploded over it. I expect it to be barf-worthy, but it's actually super delicious, and we end up eating the whole thing as we walk, pointing at performers, colorful awnings, and cute shirts and hats in store windows that we *have* to have before we leave. My heart is set on a t-shirt that says 'Keep Calm and Dragon.' Erika loves spirit jerseys, which I've never been a huge fan of, but she can't get enough of them. And while they aren't my style, I'm more than happy to encourage her to buy anything. I'm an enabler as far as shopping goes.

We reach the drawbridge which is filled with people taking selfies in front of the castle. Water cascades down a shallow river beneath the bridge, its gurgling voice adding to the natural ambiance. We decide to come back to the castle after we've dropped off our luggage. Instead of crossing the bridge, we follow a path to the left of it which leads up to two of the three resorts: The Blue Loch and the Ethereal Odin. The Fownchimer is on the other side, more secluded due to its upscale, not to mention more expensive, nature. We pass the entryway to the Ethereal Odin which is marked by a large sign with swirling letters. Pink and purple smoke seem to be rolling off of it and it has a very 'genie in the lamp' vibe. Seems cool. Maybe we'll check out the lobby later if there's time. I read that the front desk attendants are actually holographic jinni.

Further up is the entrance to The Blue Loch. The entrance to the resort has a pathway surrounded by green shrubbery, white-spotted red mushrooms, and a little lake where a Loch Ness monster, built of smooth jade, is reaching its long neck up and smiling animatedly at us, like a dog welcoming us home.

We pass under the Blue Loch's sign and head into the lobby where several students are already checking in at the reception desk. Several Villagers (what Mythos employees are referred to as) wearing white shirts, green sashes and plaid kilts operate the long reception desk. The walls are painted with rolling green hills to give the illusion that we've just stepped into medieval Scotland. The immersion is incredible, the tables are made out of black slate and there are large firepits on either side of the main sitting area of the lobby. Each hotel's design is associated with the lore behind the varying origins of the many creatures on the island. The Blue Loch fills the Celtic bucket, obviously, while the Ethereal Odin is based on Middle Eastern Lore. The Fownchimer pays homage to the great high fantasy worlds like Westeros and Middle Earth. There's even a rumored fourth resort in the works which would take inspiration from H.P. Lovecraft's stories of Cthulhu and Arkham.

We get our room keys at the reception desk and agree to meet back in the lobby in ten minutes. We then head towards opposite ends of the lobby and take separate elevators up to our rooms.

I want a minute to relax and feel the hotel bed against my back before heading out again. I also wouldn't mind exploring the room itself. I've got this weird thing for finding all the free amenities in a hotel room. But no sooner do I enter the room (which by the way feels like a

34

knight's bed chamber out of *Game of Thrones*), do I see Zach, who I've somehow forgotten I'm STILL assigned to room with.

"Hey," I say, grabbing my suitcase, which has already arrived, and rolling it over to the bed next to the window, since he's clearly taken the one closer to the door and restroom. He doesn't respond. He simply closes his suitcase, throws his backpack over his shoulder and heads for the door.

"Really?" I snap. He pauses. "We're just going to spend this whole trip rooming together and not talking?"

He takes a breath and then leaves without a word, letting the door slam behind him. I sigh and fall onto my bed, letting my rickety suitcase fall over on its side. "Asshole," I say under my breath. I allow myself a few minutes to feel shitty about everything that's transpired with Zach over the past few weeks. We used to be so close. We used to share sheet music when one of us forgot ours at home, usually him. We used to go halvsies on chocolate bars when we could barely scrounge up enough change to get one from the school's vending machine. Hell, we used to be closer than even me and Erika. Sure, Erika and I are close, but let's face it, she and I have never stayed up all night playing through *X-Men Legends* from start to finish. That bonds two people for life!

I mourn the loss of our friendship for a few minutes before taking a deep breath and replacing that feeling with excitement. I remind myself that I'll soon be hanging out with Vincent at the Kraken show. A boy who actually wants to talk to me and even called me cute!

I go to the bathroom and adjust my hair, which is always unruly. It's really coarse and goes in whatever direction it wants. Then I put some water on a washcloth and wipe away the layer of sweat on my face that built up from the short walk to the resort. I go back to the main room, grab my messenger bag and cell phone and head out the door, giving Zach's suitcase a light kick as I go. Not enough to break anything, but enough to make me feel at least a little better.

Back in the lobby I meet up with Erika. She's changed into a yellow skirt and white buttoned blouse and is wearing this wide brimmed sun hat and these sunglasses with huge lenses. In short, she looks like a model that just stepped off the pages of Teen Vogue. I hate her. I love her.

"Ready to see the Kraken?" she asks.

"That's what he said." I hate that I'm making such a cliché joke even as I say it.

"Disgusting," she says. Then she takes my arm like we're two celebrities heading into a fancy affair like the

Tony Awards or dinner at the Ritz, and we head out the front doors back into the blazing heat.

"I should have told Vincent where to meet us." I start to freak out a little, because how is he even going to find us? He literally only knows our names.

"He'll find us," Erika says. "Don't worry. If a guy likes someone enough, they always find a way. It's like that line in *Jurassic Park*. *Gays find a way*."

"It's *Life finds a way*."

"Same thing," she says, shrugging. We take the path leading further away from Town Square and the resorts which leads us to the amphitheater. From outside, it looks like we and the crowds that are gathering for the show are entering through natural arches in the side of a sandstone wall. Within these walls, the seats of the amphitheater curve around a large tank of dark murky water, the top of which looms high above us. Everyone eyes the water behind the glass with wonderment and fear, pointing anytime a shadow flashes within. The sandstone extends high over our heads like rocky fingers, casting us in dark shadows despite the blinding sunlight leaking in through cracks and seams around the amphitheater.

We shove our way into a crowded aisle and step over a bunch of other guests to get to an empty group of three seats just outside the front rows marked as 'the splash zone' because Erika is not about to let her new outfit get wrecked. I'm looking around like an idiot for Vincent but so far, he's MIA.

"Dammit," I say. "I was really hoping he'd be here. I could use some cheering up."

"Why?" asks Erika. "Are you sad? What happened?"

"Zach happened," I say.

"Oh, right, you guys are rooming together."

"I just don't want him to hate me."

"He doesn't hate you."

"Did he tell you that?"

"Well . . . no." She sighs. "He and I haven't really talked as much since you guys . . ."

"I know." Long story short, I got Erika in the divorce. And yes, that also makes me feel like crap about the whole situation.

"He just needs time," she says, trying to stay positive despite everything. "And look, don't be so worried about rooming with him. We'll spend as much time out of our rooms as possible. Trust me, I'm the Queen of denial."

I force a weak smile.

"There you guys are," says Vincent, sitting down next to me, appearing seemingly out of nowhere. He smiles at me and I swear to God I just melt into my metal seat, which is entirely possible since it's like ten thousand degrees out here.

"H-hey," I manage to say.

"Hey again," says Erika, with a wave.

"For a minute there I thought I wouldn't be able to find you guys," says Vincent.

"I knew you'd come through," says Erika, nudging me in the side.

"I'm glad you did." I feel like an idiot.

Then he puts his hand on my leg and gives it the gentlest little squeeze. "Me too."

I'm glad the music, led by a thundering bass drum roll, begins at that moment, drawing Vincent's attention towards the glass tank. I'm pretty sure I look like a deer in headlights and my cheeks must be bright red because my face is burning. Luckily no one sees any of this because our eyes are all fixed on the deep blue water ahead of us as the show begins.

THREE

Epic fanfare erupts through the amphitheater as spotlights soar over us. Everyone in the auditorium cheers but our voices are soon silenced by a low voice which sounds like an old Norwegian story-teller recounting a tale of years gone by.

"Legend tells of two great sea creatures which fought a battle to the ends of the Earth. One, the heatherback, was a great whale, as large as any island." Shadows play on the glass holding back the dark water before forming into the shape of a monstrous whale which swims from the left side of the glass to the right. "The other, a terrible monster, the largest in the sea." Shadowy tentacles reach out from the right side of the glass and though the whale tries to turn and escape, it appears to be caught in the tentacles and dragged off the side of the glass. The shadows are animations rather than actual monsters, but they still send goosebumps along my arms. I give a small shiver.

"Since the days of this legend," continues the voice,

"stories of the Kraken have permeated popular culture all the way back to the 1800's, when Alfred Tennyson published his sonnet, The Kraken."

A surly British voice interrupts the story-teller to speak a few lines from the sonnet, which I've obviously already read on Wikipedia.

"Below the thunders of the deep;
Far far beneath in the abysmal sea,
His ancient, dreamless, uninvaded sleep
The Kraken sleepeth: faintest sunlight's flee."

As he speaks, large shadowy tentacles animate themselves along the glass, thrashing about. We watch as a shadowy ship sails onto the glass, a captain at its mast barking orders silently to his crew.

"Even Ishmael of Herman Melville's novel, Moby Dick, feared the beast," says the story-teller. We watch as the ship whirls about before sailing off the side of the glass. "But until now, the creature has been only a story, a legend, a myth." Smoke begins to fill the amphitheater rolling in from behind. The audience, us included, stirs restlessly in our seats. "Now, thanks to the world-class scientists here at Mythos, the Kraken, at long last, lives. Will you join me, fellow myth seekers, in releasing it to the world?"

Everyone in the audience screams a resounding "YES!!!"

"On the count of three then," says the story-teller with an amused chuckle. "One. Two. Three."

Everyone in the audience yells the words without needing to be told them. "Release the Kraken!"

Suddenly, the whole amphitheater begins to rise, our seats lifting towards the top of the glass tank. As we reach the top, sunlight breaks into the amphitheater overtaking the shade that was previously provided by the overhanging sandstone. As we come to a halt, the smoke which has been building up, rolls out over the surface of the water which is now before us. Gentle waves play against the crags which enclose the water. To my surprise, the water seems to open into the ocean, but I'm certain they've got all sorts of containments in place beneath the surface to keep the Kraken from escaping. High above the water's surface, another tram, one which journeys to the inner parts of the park, passing over and through the varying exhibits we'll see on the tour tomorrow, speeds by on an elevated track which arcs over the water.

Across the water, a large wooden ship with billowing black sails turns the corner around the crag on the left and starts moving lazily towards us. I almost expect pirates to appear on it, waggling swords at us.

"Ladies and Gentlemen, children of all ages," chimes an announcer who sounds much younger and peppier than the story-teller. "Mythos proudly welcomes you to Kraken's Devastation, a show sure to mystify, terrify and vivify!" The whole crowd cheers as the ship approaches from afar, rocking lazily on the waves across the water's surface. I find myself glancing left and right, scanning the surface of the water for any sign of the mythical beast which waits somewhere below.

To this day, no one really knows what the 'special sauce' is that Dawson Saks discovered in order to make it possible to create these beasts. Mythos reps will smile and tell reporters it's all a matter of genomics, but leading scientists swear that no amount of genomes can make a gigantic flying dragon. They can't seem to find any other explanation though, and since no self-respecting scientist is about to admit that magic actually exists, the whole thing remains one enormous secret.

"You might be wondering what that ship is doing out there," says the announcer. "Is it a gang of pirates come to loot, pillage and steal from the fine folks gathered in the amphitheater today? Or perhaps it's some brave explorer, seeking his fortune here on Mythos Isle? No, no folks. Don't worry. We wouldn't dare put anyone, even the bravest of souls, out on these dangerous waters."

The whole audience goes quiet, because now they're doing exactly what I'm doing: scanning the water's blue surface for signs of the monster.

"For centuries, stories have been told of how the mighty Kraken ended the journeys of pirates, explorers and crusaders alike. But what drove this monster of the deep to feed on the souls of unsuspecting humans? Is it true that we taste just like chicken?"

This gets a few light chuckles from the crowd. A few too many, if you ask me.

"This was one of the many questions our scientists faced when recreating the terror of the seas. But to our surprise, the Kraken wasn't hungry for people at all! After careful study, our intrepid scientists discovered that what the Kraken actually wanted from all the ships it sank was the ships themselves. As it turns out, the Kraken gets its nutrients from wood and iron, the main ingredients in any 1800's ship. If the Kraken ever *did* exist in the wild, this might account for why Kraken attacks have gone down 100% since the dawn of the Industrial Age and the shift to steel and copper from wood as the main material for ships. Luckily for all of you, we just happen to have one such ship made to order. And that's a good thing because our Kraken, which goes by the name of Mera, is hankering for her afternoon snack!'"

A few people actually 'Aww' at this, as if a giant sea creature could ever be cute.

The announcer goes quiet and a soft note plays from a violin, heightening the suspense that already clouds the air around us. I look over and notice that Vincent is leaning forward, a keen smile on his face which makes him look like a child. I get caught up in staring at his alabaster cheeks so much that I forget to watch the ship, which has now turned and is sailing just beyond the front row of amphitheater seats and the top lip of the glass which still separates us from the water. The audience suddenly gasps collectively, and I whip my head back towards the water.

Looming over the side of the ship opposite the audience is an enormous suction-cup covered tentacle. The long arm shimmers with dark maroon hues in the sunlight as it waits patiently. I expect it to come crashing down, but instead we see another tentacle and then another. Soon, there are ten tentacles looming over the ship, surrounding it. We all wait with bated breath. Somewhere to my left, a child begins to cry, and as if on cue, the first tentacle smashes down into the center of the ship, snapping the mast like a toothpick. The sail falls sideways, billowing until it lands gently on the churning surface of the water.

Another tentacle crashes down, then another, and

another. The crunching, splintering of the wood fills our ears. From the water, two enormous crab-like legs reach up and pierce the side of the ship. Then they pull the ship down just enough that water begins to gurgle into the fresh holes in the hull. Within seconds the sea, and the Kraken, are pulling the ship under. A few moments more and the ship, half engulfed, tips on its back end, gurgles downwards, and is swallowed by the water. The amphitheater seats begin to move once more, this time lowering so that we watch as the ship is pulled into the blue depths. The water's surface bubbles and churns and then rests once more before it disappears from our line of sight.

As the seats lower, the amphitheater darkens. We watch through the glass as the ship is torn into dozens of pieces and sinks further than we can see, presumably to be swallowed up by the Kraken. The last of the ship disappears from view and the story-teller's voice returns.

"Go now and warn those who would seek their fortunes on the ocean's waves. The Kraken awaits all who dare venture too far from the safety of land." The music swells and the animated shadows play along the glass until finally settling so that they spell out "Kraken's Devastation."

The crowd goes wild, cheering and clapping as if

we've just watched some Tony winning performance. It was cool and all, but I can't help but feel a little bit horrified by what I just saw. My mind races with thoughts of what it would have been like to actually be on one of these ships downed by the Kraken. The very thought of it makes my mouth dry. Up until now I've been so excited to see all of these mythical creatures that I haven't really thought about the implications of the existence of such a park. It's the first time that I understand what a danger these creatures could pose to the world. And even though I know that the safety protocols of this park are far and away the best the world has ever seen, I can't help but think about all the 'what ifs' of this place. Surely Dawson Saks has heard of *Jurassic Park* and the dangers that come with playing God.

"That was so cool," says Vincent, turning to look at me and snapping me out of my contemplations. The seats have stopped moving and the crowd begins to shuffle as they gather up their belongings and move towards the exits, ready for the next thrill of the day.

"Yeah," I say, half-heartedly.

"Alright boys," says Erika. "I think we need a snack followed by some light shopping. Who's with me?"

"Snaaaack!" I say like I'm some zombie driven by cookies and glitter-covered popcorn.

"Mind if I tag along?" asks Vincent. "I'd love to check out the store in the Grand Palace with you."

"Of course, we don't mind," says Erika. "Right?" She nudges me, presumably to make sure I'm still on board with hanging out with this gorgeous guy who's apparently super into me.

"R-right," I say, shyly, feeling a new shade of red flush my cheeks.

"Perfect," says Vincent. He stands and then offers me his hand. I stare at it, slightly confused. "Shall we?" he asks, and for a moment I can almost imagine him as a prince at some medieval ball, asking for my hand on the dance floor. Hopefully this whole thing doesn't end with me turning into a pumpkin. I bite my bottom lip and take his hand. He gives me a light pull, helping me to my feet.

"What?" asks Erika. "No one's going to help me to my feet? Do my ankles not look weak enough?"

I laugh and bow before her, offering her my hand. "My lady," I say cordially. She takes my hand and puts the fingertips of her other hand dramatically over her gaping mouth.

"Oh! My good sir," she says.

"Mayeth I escort you to thine supper and frivolities this evening?" I ask in a British accent. Unfortunately, my British accent sounds half Jamaican and half French, so not British at all.

"You may, but I must warn thee," she says, feigning shyness. "I am but a virgin."

I burst out laughing. "Ma'am! I said supper and frivolities. Me thinks the lady doth flatter herself."

She slaps my arm. "Hater!" she yells as she laughs. She stands on her own and starts for the exit. "Come on boys, we've got some Kappa Kreme Filled Donuts to try!"

I shrug and laugh, looking at Vincent, who smiles, and with my hand in his, leads me out of the amphitheater. I know how cheesy this sounds, but it seems kind of crazy that I came all the way to a land of fairy tales to live out one of my own. I mean, back home I couldn't get any play from guys to save my life, but here I am in this amazing place, holding a boy's hand. It almost makes me wonder why I didn't come out sooner.

We head down a path that leads around to the front of the Town Square and find the little stall selling Kappa Kremes, which are green baked donuts with green tea cream filling. The top is a chocolate turtle shell with thin lines of icing drawn in a crisscrossing pattern. Vincent and I share one since he insists he isn't much of a sweets guy. He takes a bite and immediately spits it out into a little napkin, leaving the rest to me. Gross, but I guess no one is perfect. More for me!

I think the Kappa Kreme is divine. The dough is airy and sweet. The cream inside is luscious and cool on my tongue. And the chocolate shell has a light crunch to it which adds this amazing texture. Erika and I both agree, we'll need at least five more of these before the trip is over.

We also stop by the bakery, and while there are plenty of things to try, I grab a regular chocolate chip cookie. You might be wondering why I would get something so basic in a place with all sorts of new and exciting things to try. Well, let me be the first to tell you that the best way to judge any bakery is to start with the basics. If they can't get a chocolate chip cookie right, what hope does the Griffin's Claw Double-Decker Cookie Sandwich have? I bite into it and this warm gooey burst of perfection fills my mouth, littered with just the right amount of semi-sweet chocolate chips. In review, Mythos has now given me the boy of my dreams AND the cookie of my dreams. Consensus, I never want to go home.

I offer a little bit to Vincent, but he politely declines. Erika takes a bite and looks like she might cry from how good it is. We decide to head for the Grand Palace. I finish the cookie along the way, licking the remains of chocolate from each and every finger.

Erika and I somehow manage to spot Zach at the

same time. He's leaning against the outer wall of the jewelry shop where they sell personalized gem necklaces, rings and tiaras. It's clearly for higher spenders than us. I can't quite figure why Zach is even near a store like this until I see that he's talking to Janice Makfen, or as I like to call her: Richie McSnobpants. She laughs at something he's just said as if he just told the funniest joke ever. I've known Zach for a long time, and I can tell you that he isn't that funny.

"She's laying it on pretty thick," says Erika.

I roll my eyes and push forward, trying my best to ignore Zach as well as he seems to be ignoring me, which is very well.

The sun is starting to set when we finally cross the drawbridge and approach the entrance to the Grand Palace. Just as we're about to cross the threshold, Vincent pulls away, letting my hand fall out of his. I turn to see him standing just outside the entrance, which is a huge arched entryway, looking a little confused and anxious.

"Hey," I say. "You okay?"

"Sorry," he says, rubbing his left elbow with his right hand. "I just got a little freaked out."

"Freaked out?" I move closer to him with a caring smile. Dozens of guests are passing by, entering and exiting the store behind me, but right now all I see is

Vincent.

"I know I can come on a little strong," he says. "I just . . . when I saw you on the train, I instantly liked you. I just don't want you to feel like you have to hang out with me. I know your friend has sort of been pushing you to. I think you're super cute, but if you want me to leave you guys alone, I'll go."

I let out a breath and shake my head. I guess it's a weird thought to think that someone has the same anxieties that I have. I think we all know that we're all people but seeing someone else freak out about the same things I freak out about can feel a little jarring. Like, oh right, you're a human being too.

But I also feel bad, because he's taken my shyness around him as being disinterested. I move in closer to him and take his hand. Standing like this, face to face, I notice that I'm a good inch shorter than him. I look up into his eyes and smile. His eyes are like ocean waves and light reflects in shimmering flashes off of them. Staring into them, I almost forget what we were talking about or even where I am.

"I'm sorry, Vincent," I say, steadying my thoughts. "This is all just really new to me. I hope I didn't give you the wrong impression. I DO want to spend time with you. I think the fact that you came up to me on the train is amazing and brave. I could never do that if it were the other way around. I'd be too nervous."

"Yeah," says Vincent. "I actually was pretty nervous. Truth is, I still am."

"Well," I say. "Don't be. I liked it. I like . . . you."

He grins and blushes, sort of. His skin is pretty pale, so his version of blushing and mine are fairly different hues of red. "Really?"

"Really."

"So . . . you still want me to come into the Grand Palace with you?" he asks.

"Yes," I say, moving backwards over the threshold and giving him a little tug. "I want you to come in and look at shirts and hats and tell me I look good in all of them. I want you to take selfies with oversized plushies with me and buy tons of pre-wrapped snacks that we'll inevitably get sick on. Come with me."

He steps forward. "Okay." We enter the store hand in hand.

This should probably be a given at this point, but the store is far beyond anything I could have imagined. It's enormous for one. It's as if we've entered the throne room of a castle. Red carpet atop black stone leads to the varying parts of the store. There are displays filled with dragon-shaped hats and Mythos t-shirts. The walls are covered from top to bottom in unicorn, fairy and kappa plushies, which kids are snatching from the shelves and hugging tightly, proclaiming that they'll never let go. The ceiling arcs high over our heads where a pack of stuffed gryphons hang as if in mid-flight. Cash registers beep, music jingles from various toddler toys and the clickety-clack of hangars being pulled off and shoved back onto racks fills the air.

"This one," says Erika who's homed in on the spirit jerseys like a bloodhound. "I need this one," she says, grabbing a baby blue and pale purple tie-dyed spirit jersey. The back reads 'I'm a Unicorn' and there's a shimmering horn inlaid into the fabric. She drapes it over herself and looks down. "Yep," she says. "Sold."

I attempt to agree with her, but the words fall short on my tongue when behind her, I see a familiar face bustling through the crowd with two assistants in tow. Dawson Saks, owner, creator and CEO of Mythos, is here. And he's heading right for us!

FOUR

Dawson Saks was born to a German-American father and a Japanese mother, hence the non-Asian last name. Hence also the very Japanese looks. His sleek chestnut hair is combed back in a fashionably short style with a visible part on his left side. He has a short beard and mustache that appear groomed to perfection. He's lean and muscular which is shocking because you don't expect a man as busy as him to even find the time workout. He's wearing a black Michael Kors cardigan over a fitted white dress shirt with skinny black slacks and Hugo Boss shoes.

The thing is, I know that Dawson Saks is a good-looking guy. I've seen him speak on TV and YouTube probably a billion times, if you count all the re-watches. But as he walks towards me, looking down at the contents of a manila folder that's just been placed in his hands, I'm a bit taken aback at how jaw-droppingly gorgeous he is. PS: you can blame Erika for my ability to identify brand names at a glance. It's practically a prerequisite for staying friends with her.

Now I know what you're thinking: boy crazy. But this isn't a boy walking towards me at all. This is a man. A multi-billion dollar-per-year earning man. Even the lesbianest of lesbians would probably turn to gawk. Is that offensive to lesbians? I don't know. I'm still so new to all of this. At least I'm not saying it out loud.

Suddenly, Dawson is standing right in front of me. He stops, looks up and says: "Excuse us, young man." Then he smiles and the thin lines at the sides of his eyes crinkle up.

"Y-y-you're . . ." I stutter.

He lets out a laugh and one of the assistants leans forward to whisper loudly in his ear. "We really should be going," says the woman.

"Nonsense Patricia," says Dawson whose voice is smooth like silk. "This young man has something he'd like to say." He looks at me expectantly.

"You're . . . Dawson Saks," I finally say.

Erika gasps. "THE Dawson Saks?" she squeals, covering her mouth with both her hands.

"I'm . . . a huge fan," I somehow manage to blurt out.

"Sir," says the other assistant, a middle-aged balding man with thick black-rimmed glasses. He places a hand on Dawson's shoulder, but Dawson brushes the hand away as if it were a stray piece of lint. Meanwhile, Patricia has taken out her cell phone and is now speaking quickly over it, covering the receiver end with her hand in order to keep the conversation as private as possible.

"Thank you, young man," says Dawson. He reaches into the side pocket of his cardigan and pulls out a circular card, which he hands to me. I take it and look down to see that it has his autograph already on it. "Now, be sure to have the most fun at my park that you possibly can, alright?"

I nod vigorously. Out of the corner of my eye I can see Erika nodding as well.

"This is a place where dreams and magic come to life, so you must take advantage of it before you have to go back to school . . ." he yawns dramatically as if the very thought is putting him to sleep. "And homework, and books . . . and . . . studying . . ." He closes his eyes and slumps his body, then actually starts to snore. We both laugh and his eyes pop back open once more.

"Sir, we really must—" says Patricia, who has placed her hand over her cell phone so that the person on the other end can't hear her.

"Get a grip on yourself, Patricia," snaps Dawson. "We'll find it, okay? This sort of thing happens every day and every day it turns out to be just fine. The park is safe and secure, unlike your job here if you interrupt me one more time."

Patricia understandably cowers away, turning to nod and smile curtly at passersby who have taken notice of Dawson's small outburst. Even Erika and I recoil in surprise.

Dawson turns back to us, and his smile returns as if nothing has happened. "Oh, of course," he says, pulling out another circular autograph card and handing it to Erika. She takes it with the slightest hesitation.

Thinking of Vincent, I add: "Oh, can we get one for . . ." I turn to point to him, but I don't see him anywhere.

"Right, well, off we go," says Dawson. He points back at us as he and his two assistants walk away. "Remember now. Wonderful time. Lots of fun. Magic and dreams and all that." Erika waves and nods to him as he blends into the crowd and then disappears through a door that's painted so that it looks like part of the wall.

I don't wave to Dawson Saks, my hero, because I'm spinning around searching the crowd for Vincent. "Did you see where he went?" I ask Erika.

"Where who went?" she says. "Dawson Saks? You didn't see him go through that secret door?"

"No," I say. "Vincent."

She looks around, suddenly noticing that he's gone.

"The hell?" she says. "He was here a second ago."

"Right?" And then a horrible thought dawns on me. "Do you think he freaked out about how fangirl I got when I saw Dawson Saks?"

Erika scoffs. "That makes no sense. He's Dawson-fucking-Saks. I fangirled and I'm nowhere near the level of nerd that you are."

"Rude."

"Is it really rude if it's a fact?"

"Yes."

"Fair enough." She pushes a hand through her hair. "Maybe he saw a sale on dragon plushies?"

"Erika, it's Mythos. They don't do sales. Everything is expensive all the time." I'm still searching the crowd but it's no use. I bury my head in my hands and put my back up against a display holding an array of notebooks themed after the various magical creatures on the island with a bold Mythos logo stamped on the front. "I should have been more chill," I groan.

"Noooo," says Erika sarcastically. "Mr. 'OMG DID YOU HEAR ABOUT THE JONAS BROTHERS REUNION?' Yeah, you're the master of the chill."

"Outside, he was freaking out and telling me that he thought I didn't like him because I wasn't acting as into him as he was into me," I say.

"That's not true. You're just super shy!" says Erika because of course she knows that. She's my best friend. My sister from another mister. Thing 2 to my Thing 1.

"Yeah, but he didn't know that, so he thought I was, I don't know, annoyed by him or something." I'm freaking out, wondering if people would think I've gone crazy if I just started slapping myself. "And now he just saw what I look like when I'm fangirling, and he probably thinks that if I don't act like that with him then maybe I'm not that into him."

"Woah, woah, woah. Take a breath." Erika wraps her arms around my shoulders and hugs me tightly. "Henry Lau. You are the sweetest guy I know. I'm sure we'll run into him again and you can explain everything. It's not like this is some chance encounter. We go to the same school. Worst case scenario, you can just corner him at his locker *Riverdale* style."

"Yeah," I say, hugging her back. "You're probably right."

"Probably right? I am extremely right. And don't you forget it."

I laugh.

"It's getting late and our tour starts early in the morning," she says. "I want to bring a bag tomorrow, but not these bags." She points beneath her eyes. I roll my own eyes because this is not the first time she's told me some version of this joke. But I laugh anyway because, I'll admit it, the girl knows how to work a punchline. She takes my arm once more and we head back towards the store's entrance. I spot a few things that I will for sure need to come back to buy before we head back out into the night. Some souvenirs mostly.

It's perfect timing because when we get outside the fireworks show over the castle is just starting. We grab a spot on the curb of Town Square and look up above the castle as burning blasts of red, green, gold and blue fill the air. The show is accompanied by a sweeping orchestral soundtrack, and several of the fireworks actually create complete imagery like trees, mountains and mythical creatures to tell a story. There's a dragon, a hippogriff, and then a unicorn. What's more amazing is that the images the fireworks create actually animate as if they are exploding to life right before our eyes. They're like the fireworks Gandalf made in *The Lord of the Rings* but in real life and 100 times better.

A couple of fireworks go off and form what looks like a dwarf and a gnome skipping off to work with their pickaxes in tow.

"I didn't realize they had things like dwarves and gnomes here," says Erika. "I thought they were all animals."

"They are," I say, not taking my eyes off the show. "Rumors say that they discussed making mythical beings with higher brain development early on but realized it wouldn't be ethical to keep them in captivity. So, they left the idea on the drawing board. No animal on Mythos Isle has an intelligence beyond that of a dolphin."

"What about fairies?" she asks. "Aren't they, like, little glowing people?"

"Apparently they're not," I say. "I hear the fairies here are more like insects. One vlogger I follow compared them to wasps with baby faces."

"That's horrifying," she says in disgust.

"I know," I say with a smile plastered on my face.

The grand finale of the show involves about a hundred fireworks, fireballs and flat-out explosions which are hurled into the sky and culminates in them combining to form a massive dragon that flies up, swoops down on us, and pulls up so that it soars over our heads, back along the central street and out of sight. The music swells around us and makes the finale of the show feel even more beautiful. The crowd goes wild with cheers. I know how weird this sounds, but I've actually managed to shed a few tears. Consider me impressed.

We get up and head back to the resort. I say

goodnight to Erika in the lobby and we hug. I love that she's such a good hugger. Some people just don't get it, but Erika's hugs have a very precise pressure to softness ratio, and they last long enough to be comforting but not so long that they ever feel awkward. They're perfect. Back in my room I find that Zach hasn't returned yet. That's fine, because I'm not about that silent treatment life.

I change into teal cotton shorts and an old sleeveless black shirt and crawl under the covers of the soft bed. I pull out my phone and go to Instagram to see if I can hunt down Vincent. Usually I'm pretty good at the Instastalking game, but tonight I must be off because I can't find him anywhere. I check the pages of the couple of band kids I follow and can't seem to find him in any of the group photos. Maybe he's new? I can't help but realize that I know so little about him. But maybe that's how relationships work. Maybe you fall head over heels for each other right away and then fill in all the details as you go. I like the idea of getting to know more about Vincent. I wonder if he and I have any of the same obsessions. Does he play *Pokémon Go*? Does he stalk the Instagram pages of every single Mythos vlogger in the world? Does he like authentic Korean bar food? And if he isn't into it, is he at least prepared to try it? I'm a pretty adventurous eater, and I'd love to be able to share that with someone.

I lose myself in thinking about all of this and imaging all the cute-couple pictures we'll post when we get home. I settle in, ready to end the night with a smile on my face just as the door flies open and slams into the wall. I sit up with lightning speed because for all I know an axe murderer has just invaded my room.

"What the hell?" I yell before I see two familiar faces stumbling in. Zach and Janice are red in the face when they pull their lips apart long enough to look at me with befuddled eyes.

"Henry?" asks Zach. "What the hell are you doing here?" I notice he's slurring his words, and I suddenly feel really pissed, because how did they even manage to get a hold of liquor in a place like this where rules and regulations are everything.

"Are you drunk?" I ask angrily.

"Are you?" he asks, and Janice starts giggling because apparently this girl with her perfectly curled blond-highlighted hair and flawless brown skin will laugh at anything.

"Did you not think I'd be in here?" I ask, pulling my legs out from under the covers and standing up. "What was your plan? Were you just going to have sex in the bed next to me while I was asleep?"

"Excuse me?" says Janice, attitude rolling across her

64

face like an incoming storm. "I am a lady." She pauses and flips her hair. "I'd prefer if we could refer to it as 'making love.'"

"Holy shit," I say. Is this actually happening right now?

"Come on Zach," she says, pulling on his arm. "We can go to my room. Daddy upgraded me to a single so I wouldn't have to deal with inconsiderate roommates."

"Of course he did," I snap.

"What the hell is your problem?" growls Zach.

"My problem?" I snarl back. "My problem is that you won't even talk to me."

"Yeah, it fucking sucks, doesn't it!" he yells, and we all fall silent. He's clearly angry, but in his eyes I can see the same look he had when we found out we wouldn't be in the same homeroom class in fourth grade. Our first year apart. Zach may be yelling, but deep down, I think he might actually be . . . sad?

"What are you . . .?" But I'm too late. Zach scoffs and is already stalking off with Janice close behind.

"Forget it," he says as he leaves, slamming the door behind them.

"What a spaz attack," I hear Janice say in the hallway.

"Whatever," says Zach and then they're gone.

I flop backwards onto the bed and grab one of the

enormous pillows, shoving it over my face so that I can yell into it. The pillow muffles the sound. Then I throw it across the room before rolling over. I toss and turn, mulling over what's become of my friendship with Zach since coming out. I can't help but hope that things with Vincent will be so good that they'll outweigh all the shit with Zach. If I ever see him again. He keeps disappearing. Here's to hoping. Sometime around two in the morning, I finally fall asleep.

When I wake up, the alarm on my phone is playing one of my favorite songs—"Waving Through A Window" from *Dear Evan Hansen*—and the sun is peeking through the window shades, making me squint as my vision adjusts. I roll over to see that Zach's bed is still untouched. Well, at the very least this means he got some action with Janice last night, which hopefully means he's in a better mood. Sex puts people in a better mood, right? That's what I've heard anyway. It's not like I can speak from experience.

I get up and shower then fix my hair which of course takes forever. By the time I throw on my "There be dragons here" purple V-neck, I'm already running late to meet Erika in the lobby. I grab my messenger bag which is filled with snacks, my notebook, and a few other essentials, and head out.

Erika shows up in the lobby just as I do, which makes

sense because if I take forever to look like this, then she probably woke up at the crack of dawn in order to look like *that*. She's wearing yellow shorts and a loose grey featherweight shirt which hangs off one shoulder. Her hair is curling down to her shoulders and she's wearing a baseball cap. This is casual Erika. She's sporty and cute and even though it all looks thrown together, I'm sure every piece of the outfit was meticulously planned from the hat down to her Doc Martin boots.

"Ready to see a dragon?" I ask enthusiastically.

"I bet you ask all the boys that," she says slyly.

"Ugh. Don't get me started on boys."

"What? Why? You love boys."

"Between Vincent flaking on me and Zach showing up mid-sex with Janice Makfen at our room last night, I could use a boy-free day. I'm on sabbatical from boys."

"Yeah, we'll see how long that lasts," says Erika as we head for the door.

"What's that supposed to mean?" I ask as the doors slide automatically open and the warm outside air absorbs us. Other students from our class are already making their way down the path to the Town Square where we'll all be catching the sky train that makes the journey around the entire island for today's tour.

"Nothing," she says, and I can tell she's regretting her

comment.

"Come on, just tell me," I insist.

"Henry, you know I love you," she says like a mother talking to their kid who just failed their first test.

"That sounds ominous," I say.

"But you've gone a little boy crazy since you came out. You're constantly fawning over guys now. I mean, look at you and Vincent. You just met and you're already kind of obsessed with him. I know he's hot, but what else do you know about him?"

"What the hell?" Erika is supposed to be the one person in my life who supports me regardless of how crazy or childish I behave. We're both supposed to have each other's back no matter what. No. Matter. What.

"Forget it," she says as we turn onto the downhill path. "Forget I said anything. I'm not trying to criticize, I just . . ."

"You just what?"

"I just want you to be a little more careful," she says, and I can tell she's being genuine. I want to be pissed at her, but her words aren't coming from a place of hate or anger. She's really worried about me. But for some reason knowing that makes me feel worse. "Guys are wired to hurt you if you let them. I'm not saying Vincent's a bad guy. I'm really not. I'm just saying you should get to know him a little more before you decide he's worth your time. He ran off last night and you looked heart broken. I can't imagine how much it will hurt you if he actually does something really shitty."

I take a few seconds to process what Erika is saying. "Look," I finally say. "I appreciate your concern, but you don't know what it's like to come out and feel all alone and then finally have someone pay attention to you like that. *All* the guys pay attention to you. You're attractive and confident and awesome. I am none of those things. On top of that, even if you meet someone who is gay, then there's the hurdle of whether they're even into Asian guys. Gay or straight, most people aren't, unless they have some fetish. So, when someone actually likes me, I have to see where it goes."

Erika stops and turns me by my shoulders so that I'm staring into her eyes. I feel every muscle in my body begging to turn away because I hate this sort of intense eye contact. "You listen to me. Henry Lau is my best friend."

"Why are you talking to me like I'm not me?" I ask, which is a pretty confusing question to be asking.

"He's my best friend, so don't you ever talk about him like that. He is just as attractive and awesome and worthy of love and affection as me and then some. So, start treating him like it." She lets me go and then raises her eyebrows in a defiant way before turning, sticking her nose up and runway walking down the path.

It's weird to think that Erika just defended me from myself. And as much as I want to be angry with her for stepping into my business, I can't because, holy shit, she's singularly the most wonderful person in my life.

I sigh and follow after her. When I catch up, we side-eye each other and smile stupidly the way families do at Thanksgiving dinner after Grandma just farted . . . again.

"So," she says awkwardly. "Zach and Janice huh?"

"Don't remind me," I grumble, shaking my head to fight off the returning images of them wrapped up in each other's arms.

"Their babies would be hideous," she says. I burst out laughing.

"Only you would think about that," I say.

"What? Knowing how hot someone's babies will be is important!"

The path leads us back to Town Square. From there, we follow the sign next to the ice cream shop to get to a ramp which leads us to the sky train terminal, specifically looking out for the Nebula, which is the train that embarks on the island tour. Unlike the Comet, the Nebula's seats face the exterior of the train. The walls and ceiling of each of the adjoining four cars are made of a super thick reinforced glass allowing for easy viewing of all the mythical creatures we'll hopefully be seeing today. We grab a seat just as Mr. Zeckel gets on board. He's got a big black shoulder bag and is wearing a Hawaiian shirt, khaki shorts, hiking boots, and a big fisherman's hat. He's out of breath and is only able to manage waving to the kids sitting just inside the train's door; sunblock and sweat drip thickly down his nose.

Zach and Janice arrive soon after, arm in arm and giggling. Zach is wearing this enormous tooth on a black string around his neck. It looks like some sort of prehistoric bling.

"Cool necklace," says Mr. Zeckel. For the record, if a teacher thinks something you're wearing is 'cool' you should probably take it off and burn it.

"Thanks, Mr. Zeckel," says Zach.

"I bought it for him," says Janice proudly. "It's a real razor-back dragon tooth. Supposedly we'll see one today."

"Cool *and* educational," says Mr. Zeckel. "I like it."

I spot new kid Noah out of the corner of my eye and just happen to catch him rolling his eyes at the exchange. He catches me looking though, which is painfully awkward. He stares back at me and raises one eyebrow questioningly. I try to cover it up by pulling my phone from my pocket and staring at it, but the damage has already been done. I nod as if I've just read something I agree with which is ridiculous since the screen is still blank. If there was a hole I could crawl into and hide right now, I would.

Zach and Janice sit near the front of the train car near Thomas Ruiz who's flirting with yet another girl who seems to think he's funnier than he is. This guy. A whole bunch of other kids from our class as well as a bunch of families get on the train.

The conductor sits in a little compartment near the front. He's a heavier set man with gray hair and a walrus mustache. He's wearing a dapper purple suit and cap. "Welcome aboard everyone. The Nebula will be leaving the station shortly, bound for places unknown. In the meantime, make sure to get settled and place your belongings underneath the seat. Keep your camera's out though."

I glance sideways, this time more carefully, at Noah. He's wearing a white and grey striped t-shirt with the same holes-in-the-knees black jeans, not to mention his staple, the metal-grey beanie. How anyone can wear a beanie in this heat, I'll never know. Much like the last time I saw him, he's got earbuds in. Clearly, he's super excited about today's expedition. Not. Something tells me that if he was allowed to, he'd stay in his room all day. But Mr. Zeckel has assured us there will be a quiz on this tour when we get back, so he's here . . . barely.

I peer around the train car but see no sign of Vincent, which super sucks. I know I wanted a boy-free day, but I was at least hoping to clear some things up with him. And let's be honest, what gay guy says they want a boy-free day and actually means it? His absence does seem a little strange though.

"I don't see Vincent," I nudge Erika hoping she can point him out. She scans the train but gives up and shrugs.

"Guess he's doing the afternoon tour."

"Afternoon tour?"

"Yeah," she says as if everyone knew there was such a thing. "We could do the morning one or the afternoon one. I chose this one so we could shop all afternoon."

"And why did I choose this one?" I ask, hoping she can recall what I've apparently let fall out of my brain.

"Because you were 'sick' when we had to sign up." She uses her fingers to put air quotes around the word 'sick.' "So, I signed us both up." I wasn't actually 'sick.' I took two days off of school when I came out to my parents. It was just a tough time and I needed a couple days to regroup. But damn, if I'd known I would miss signing up for Mythos trip events, I would have saved coming out for another week.

"Alright everyone," announces the conductor, interrupting our conversation. His voice echoes through the speakers located over our heads so we can hear him as clearly as if he were seated right next to us. "On behalf of Mythos I'd like to welcome you to the Nebula Sky Tour. Today we'll be taking a closer look at the many mythical beasts which call Mythos Isle their home. I expect lots of 'Oos' and 'Awes' but if you dive in deeper, you'll find there's also plenty to learn along the way." The doors close as a few of us, myself included, groan at the thought of learning. "Don't worry. If you happen to gain some newfound knowledge, it'll be our little secret. We expect our journey into the unknown to go smoothly today, but in the unlikely event of an emergency . . ."

He launches into emergency protocols, but his voice fades into the background when I begin to search the train car for Vincent again. I can picture his eyes in my mind, and I yearn to find them in the crowd. It's almost like I'm a little addicted to them. Every time I let my mind wander, there they are, reminding me that he's not here. I notice that Noah is once again staring at me. What the hell is up with this guy? I avoid eye contact like the plague, but this guy can't seem to get enough. It's so awkward. I do my best to ignore him, making sure my eyes skip over the place where he's sitting as I scan the packed train.

After a slight jolt, the train starts moving. We leave the station and curve around the perimeter of Town Square where festivities and live musical performances have already started for the day. The train car leans upwards as we ascend the arc which crosses over the Kraken Amphitheater. It isn't until we're halfway over the seafront which hosts the show that the car comes to a sudden halt, throwing us all forward. There are several gasps from our fellow passengers.

"What the—" Erika has to reach up to keep her hat from falling off. "Anyone every teach this guy how to break?"

"I did hear there are a few surprises on the tour," I say. "Maybe we get to watch the Kraken show from up here?" I've ridden enough amusement park rides to not be too affected by operators who are heavy-footed with the breaks. Compared to some of the other people on the train, I'm pretty relaxed. That is, until the gentle hum of the engine below us goes silent.

FIVE

People all around us murmur anxiously. I can actually feel the tension thickening the air. The fact that we're in an enclosed glass box doesn't help either. I feel like every structural detail of the train stands out ten times more to me now. Since the seats are back to back facing towards the glass walls on either side, there isn't a whole lot of room to move around. The train cars, of which there are four, are only separated by accordion style bellows which are transparent just like the glass except for the fact that they can move with the train as it turns along the track. There's no way this train and its four cars were not built with the purpose of keeping their passengers in and the beasts out.

We chose to sit near the back, apart from most of the kids in our class who are huddled in their clicks along the second and third cars ahead of us, but now, I wish we were a bit closer to them. It feels as if I've willingly stepped into a trap. The cold fingers of claustrophobia tighten around my chest. I squeeze my messenger bag against my chest to help relieve some of the tension coursing through me.

"What's going on?" asks Erika, looking around our train compartment to see if anyone else might provide some sort of answer.

"Ladies and Gentlemen," starts the conductor. He yells down the train at us because the speakers are useless now that the power is out. "Please remain calm. We appear to be experiencing a loss of power. I'm going to engage our manual override and we'll be up and running shortly. No need to panic."

"The monorail at Disney goes down all the time," I say, not sure who I'm trying to assure, Erika or myself.

Erika looks at me. "I'm sure it'll be fine," she says. "But you look super pale. Are you okay?"

"Sure," I say, hoping the lie is convincing. Important me-fact: when I was little, I got trapped on a roller coaster and it totally freaked me out for life. I don't really talk about it with people because, well, it's not something that affects my life on a day to day basis, but right now I sort of wish Erika knew because then she might understand why my palms are sweating and the blood is draining from my face. "I'm fine," I say, which I think we all know is the universal way of saying: I AM TOTALLY NOT FINE!

She rubs my arm gently. "Relax hun."

I close my eyes and take a long deep breath through

my nose, hold it, and then let it out through my mouth slowly. It actually makes me feel a little bit calmer. I open my eyes and smile at Erika, hoping she can sense my newfound Zen. She smiles back sympathetically. I can't help but notice that everything seems a little darker, like the way the world shifts in color when a cloud passes lazily overhead.

In what feels like slow motion, I turn my head to look out the window in front of us. From this angle I don't recognize the tentacle which stands erect just outside, blocking out the sun behind it. But as the massive suction-cup covered arm comes towards us like a battering ram, everything clicks into place. I move left, grabbing Erika around the waist and pulling her with me so that we slam into the floor of the train car just as the glass cracks, splinters and then shatters. The tentacle wraps around the train car and quickly constricts, destroying the reinforced glass and crushing the seats we were in only moments ago.

The deafening crashing noises are suddenly replaced by screams of terror as passengers attempt to move around the tight space, attempting to get out of the tentacle's reach. Erika and I are crawling along the floor, trying our best not to be stepped on as people lunge over us and the seats beside us, heading away from the tentacle towards the back. I feel a rush of pain as someone steps on my left hand. I let out a guttural scream as a horrifying crunch alerts me to what will most likely be broken bones. I swallow the scream in an audible gulp. I can't think about the pain right now. I have to focus on how we're going to escape.

"Are you okay?!" I yell at Erika crawling beside me. She reaches up and uses the cushioned chair to stand up, pulling me to my feet by the back of my shirt.

"Yeah," she says, breathing heavily. "You?"

"I think my hand is broken," I say, nursing it. It's throbbing with pain and already swelling.

We both turn to see the tentacle crushing our previous seats like a boa constrictor tightening around its prey. "Could be worse," she says. "You could've had your *everything* broken."

People on the other side of the tentacle separating our car in half are moving further towards the front of the train. Erika and I are among the few people who are still trapped on the back end of the last train car. Mr. Zeckel and the conductor are desperately trying to get everyone to remain calm, including the other adults on the train. But that's easier said than done when you're the subject of a Kraken attack. I look forward just as another tentacle slams into the train at the joint between cars 3 and 4. We tumble forward, using parts of the windows and chairs that are still intact to keep upright.

"Shit!" yells Erika. "This is not good!"

The back end of our car suddenly lurches downwards at an angle. The Kraken has apparently decided to pull the train off of the track and car four has volunteered as tribute.

"We need to get to the next car!" I yell.

"Are you insane?" says a woman on the other side of the seats from us. She looks like she's mid-30's, mid-height, and mid-panic attack. "What are we gonna do about that?" She flails her hands in the direction of the two tentacles currently barring our path. "You can't just crawl over them!"

"We have to," says Erika. "Or we're gonna be fish food."

"Technically the Kraken is part of the squid family," I offer.

"Not the time or the place, Henry," snaps Erika.

"Sorry," I say. The car gives another lurch, placing us at an even sharper angle. "Okay, no more talking. You're right. We need to go."

"We can't!" yells the woman, making no attempt to move with us. Erika and I don't stop though. We climb, using the chairs as hand holds, to move up through the car. There are two more guys behind us also using the chairs to climb, but one of them is older and is sweating bullets. Judging by the Santa-like belly on him, I'd say this is the most physical exertion he's had in a while. The other guy is younger and wearing a baseball cap, a polo and khakis. He's wearing crocs! But even that doesn't mean he deserves to be eaten by the Kraken.

We're almost to the first tentacle when the sound of metal rending and the bellows ripping rings in our ears. The second tentacle tears through the bellows, pulling a chunk out of the train and the track below which falls out of sight, separating cars 3 and 4. Moments later, we hear the kerplunk of the water below as train parts crash to its surface. The car jolts again. Erika and I look at each other and take off running. There is a huge gap between Car 4 and Car 3; a huge gap between us and the rest of the train. And despite this turn of semi-good luck, because now we only have one tentacle to contend with to get to safety, time is definitely not on our side. Erika vaults over the first tentacle. I close my eyes and follow behind, trying not to think about the slippery surface of the tentacle as my hand grazes it.

As I land on the opposite side, the woman behind us screams. I open my eyes and turn back to see a tentacle crashing right through the window next to her, slamming into her and then showing her out the other side of the car. Her screams fade until we can no longer hear her.

"Fuck!" I'm not a huge fan of the word but what else do you say in a moment like this. Erika reaches the gap between our car and the rest of the train first and jumps to safety. Several other students as well as Mr. Zeckel pull her in. I'm about to jump too, but the train car lurches once more and I stumble backwards, grabbing onto the splintered edge of the car preventing myself from falling back down the length of the train, which is now almost perpendicular to the water below. My left-hand flares with pain causing me to let go. Now I'm dangling by only my right hand. I look down—trying to find a place to put my flailing feet—and see the larger man lose his footing and fall down into the other man with the crocs. Together, they slam into the new tentacle, and crash into the very back end of the train car. The first tentacle pulls and rips the back half of the train car away. I watch it fall, taking the two men with it.

I'm fully expecting to see it hit the water's surface, but instead my view is consumed by the Kraken itself. Unlike the show we saw yesterday, I can now see the terrifying monster in all its glory. Its mouth, filled with dozens of teeth spiraling down its throat like the inside of a massive meat grinder, is at the epicenter of its ten tentacles which are all whipping around in the air as they assault the Nebula. It has pale eyes on either side of its head which emerges from the biggest shell I've ever seen. It's a spiral shell like the ones a hermit crab might use, but gigantic. Sharp spikes protrude along the shell's spine. On the underside of the creature there are four huge claws which resemble a crab's except much, much bigger. They reach up, clawing at the air as if eager for their turn to attack the Nebula and the passenger's within.

The mouth grinds the lower half of the train car, devouring it like a blender. I close my eyes, because the last thing I want to see is the looks on the two men's faces as they're eaten alive by the Kraken. Even all the way up here, I can hear the crunching, mulching noises of the train car being ground to scraps.

"Henry!" yells Erika from the other side of the enormous gap between us. I snap out of my terror long enough to pull myself up so that I'm looking across the gap at the other students and passengers. The train track below me is all but destroyed and my train car is hanging on by a thread. If I've got any chance of surviving this, it's now or never.

I climb up onto the ledge, stepping onto the midsection of the torn-in-half train and try not to look down as the car groans loudly beneath me. To my left and right, two tentacles are swaying gently through the air, as if biding their time, considering their next move. I take a deep breath and prepare to jump—now! But I don't go. I can't. I'm frozen in fear because I'm afraid of heights, and I'm afraid of falling, and I'm mostly afraid of the giant meat grinder waiting to devour me below.

"Henry!" Erika calls out to me. She's crying now, causing her mascara to streak down her face.

I can't do this. It hits me like a ton of bricks. I cannot do this. I was not built for this. I'm not some action star or video game hero who can jump from one precarious falling structure to another. I'm not Chris Pratt, though the thought of him does relax me a little bit. I'm just Henry. No chill, bad at sports, boy crazy Henry. I'm just Henry and I cannot do this. The utter feeling of defeat rips through me and sends a single tear down my cheek.

The car groans loudly and I feel it lurching beneath me. The world seems to slow as a new voice calls to me. "Henry, jump!" it yells. And to my surprise, I do. I bend my knees and then lunge forward, kicking off the dangling train just as it falls towards the water and the Kraken's waiting mouth.

For a moment it's like a dream. I'm just flying through the air. I'm literally defying gravity! Elphaba from *Wicked* would be so proud. It's peaceful and serene and I wish I could do it forever. I extend my hands just as I begin to fall.

A hand reaches out and grabs mine, pulling me to safety. My left hand flares with pain, but I barely feel it, probably due to the intense adrenaline pulsing through me at this point.

It isn't until my shoes hit the level train car that I look up and realize that the person who called out to me, the person who caught my hand, is Noah. He stares at me with his emerald eyes, and even though I hate eye contact, I can't bring myself to look away.

Below me, the floor rumbles as the train returns to life. Red luminescent lights come on overhead. The train lurches forwards and we all grab onto each other to steady ourselves. After all, one wrong move and we could be falling right out of the open train car. We all turn to see the Kraken's tentacles swinging after us. But we're finally moving away now and he's not fast enough to catch us as we descend the arc over the water. The monster, the amphitheater and the now broken train line fade into the distance.

"God dammit, Henry!" yells Erika, throwing her arms around me. "When I say jump, you fucking jump!"

I let out a breath that I feel like I've been holding for a lifetime and hug her back. "Oh my God. Those people," I say through my heavy breaths. "Those poor people. They all . . . they're all . . ." I look back at Noah. He pulls his hand out of mine but doesn't look away.

"Thank you," I try to say, but end up only mouthing the words as no sound comes out.

He nods and finally turns away towards the front of the train. People are super packed into the remaining three cars, now that we're missing a fourth of the train. Everyone looks shell shocked.

Mr. Zeckel puts his large hand on my shoulder and gives it a gentle, reassuring squeeze. "You alright, Henry?"

"Yeah," I manage to say, finally finding my voice again. "I survived a Kraken and all I got was this lousy broken hand," I say, looking at my hand which is turning a very nasty shade of blue. "That's what the t-shirt I'm going to make will say." I try to laugh, but it comes out as tears. *Those people . . . All gone . . . All . . .*

"You're a fool," says Erika, ruffling my hair. She smiles but tears are streaming down her face. "For a minute I thought you were going to end up like . . ." *Alive only moments ago and now gone.* She doesn't have to say it. We're both thinking the same thing.

"Let's take a look at that," says Mr. Zeckel. He gingerly turns my hand from side to side, which hurts like hell. "Banged up pretty good I'd say. Probably a fracture or two." He unzips his backpack and pulls out a rolled-up cloth bandage from a preassembled first-aid kit, which he unrolls and wraps around my hand. Even that hurts. Leave it to Mr. Zeckel to be prepared for literally anything. He fastens the bandage in place and checks that it's secure. "Won't do much but should help until we can get to a doctor."

"Thanks," I say.

"Come on," he says, and we follow him.

We all move in so we're not standing right beside the open end of the train. There are open fields and trees outside now, but I can't bring myself to look out. I also can't help wondering why we haven't stopped yet. Does the conductor think we might still be in danger? The amphitheater must be at least a mile back by now. I just want to sit down and collect myself, but as we pass Zach who's got Janice wrapped around him like a scared puppy, I hear him say something that unnerves me all over again.

"Why are we speeding up?"

"Are we?" asks Janice, whose face is streaked with tears.

Zach was the first of us to get a car, an old Mustang that he and his Dad rebuilt. He'd recognize the feeling of a vehicle speeding up better than any of us. I look over at him and see his eyes shifting back and forth, as if he's figuring out a complex math problem.

"Yes," says Zach, pulling away from her. "We definitely are." He starts to squeeze through people, moving towards the front car with Janice struggling to keep up. For some reason, I follow after him. I can't explain why. Maybe it's the shock or maybe it's the need to focus on anything other than the fact that I was almost a Kraken's breakfast. *All dead.*

"Where are you going?" asks Erika in disbelief.

"I'm following Zach," I say. As if that should be enough.

"Why?" she asks, following close behind me. I glance back to see that Noah and Mr. Zeckel are with us too.

"Because he's right," I say. "There's something wrong. The conductor hasn't said anything, but We're moving uncomfortably fast. And getting faster by the second. It all feels . . . wrong. We should be stopping, or at least taking it slow. This train has taken a ton of damage. We shouldn't be getting further from Town Square and deeper into the park. But . . . we are."

"Maybe the conductor knows a safe area for security to pick us up," says Mr. Zeckel. "He does know this park better than any of us Mr. Lau." Jesus, what I really don't need right now is Mr. Zeckel trying to teach me a lesson.

I ignore him as we move through the crowd until we catch up to Zach who's leaning into the conductor's compartment at the front of the first car, having a frantic debate with the conductor.

"What the hell do you mean?" asks Zach. "Just stop it. Hit the brakes. Cut the power. Anything."

"I tried all that," says the conductor who seems more than a little stressed out. He's fiddling with every nob, lever and switch on the control panel but to no avail. It's as if the Nebula has grown a mind of its own. We're speeding along the elevated train track high above a tropical forest. In the distance ahead of us, I notice an enormous segmented-glass dome approaching.

"What is that?" I ask, pointing ahead. Everyone in our little crew turns as one to see the dome, which is growing larger by the second as we approach it.

"Shit," says the conductor.

"Sir," says Mr. Zeckel condescendingly. "Don't you think we ought to watch the language around the kids?"

"Shit! Shit! Shit!" yells the conductor, pulling on several levers which makes no difference.

"Sounds like he doesn't think we should watch our language around the kids," says Zach dryly. God, I miss his sarcastic sense of humor so much. But now is not the time to dwell on what's been lost between the two of us.

I think back to the map of the park that hangs on my bedroom wall, trying to place where we are in relation to the dome ahead of us. The park has three dome enclosures for various types of flying creatures. One is, of course, for the dragons, but we shouldn't be anywhere near that yet. It's a big part of the second half of the tour. The other is for gryphons, hippogriffs and other friendly mammal/bird hybrids. But that one should also be near the end of the tour. So that leaves the third enclosure.

"The Roc Cliffs," I say under my breath.

"Rock cliffs?" asks Erika. "You mean they built that whole thing for some mountains?"

"No, no," I correct her. "Roc. Like the giant eagles that save Frodo and Sam."

"Heroic eagles," says Mr. Zeckel. "Nothing to worry about."

"Except when the park bred them, they discovered that they're anything but friendly," I add. "They're like sky raptors. They hunt in packs and their mean as—"

"Shit!" yells the conductor, whose face has gone red.

"What he said," adds Zach.

"Still, no need to worry," adds Thomas Ruiz who's standing behind us because where else would he be when no one wants him? "The sky trains are all protected by an electromagnetic field which shocks any creature that gets too close."

"We're running on emergency systems," snaps the

conductor. "We're off the grid. A literal battery in the train is propelling us forward."

"As impressive as that is," says Thomas, "I fail to see how that pertains to anything I just . . ."

"We don't HAVE an electromagnetic field around us right now! If we did, it would have stopped the Kraken and we wouldn't be in this mess!" growls the conductor.

"Oh," says Thomas, turning pale.

The conductor stops scrambling, looks up and realizes that we're about to slam into the first of two steel-framed gates which are built to keep the rocs in their dome. The train is supposed to enter the first, wait for it to close, and then proceed through the second. We're about to do a fast-forwarded version of this with far more noise, pain and tossing about the train car.

"Everyone!" yells the conductor. "Brace yourselves!" We all do our best to grab onto each other, the walls, and the seats. A second later, the train collides with the first gate, exploding through the double doors like a battering ram. I have a brief second to take a breath and hope that the collision helped to slow the train. Passengers and students cry out all down the train. Erika is clinging to me and a nearby chair. She thought she was going to lose me earlier. I saw it in her eyes. Now, it's like she isn't ever going to let me out of her sight.

Zach is holding onto the back of the conductor's seat with Janice wrapped around his other arm. Thomas has somehow pinned himself against a wall, pushing his feet against a seatback.

Noah is . . . Noah has his arms wrapped around my chest, holding me in place. The realization hits me like a train hitting the security gate, and I'm pretty much an expert in how much force that is at this point. I want to ask him what he's thinking but there isn't time. He lets me go as soon as we're past the second gate. I want to think that the danger is passed, but as far as I can tell the train hasn't even begun to slow down. On top of that, we're now barreling over a pastel red rocky landscape made up of canyons and crags, any of which could be hiding the vicious rocs.

They don't wait to make their presence known. There's a loud screech outside which echoes over the hum of the train. "Here they come!" yells the conductor.

We look out the front window to see a flock of birds coming towards the train. At first, they could easily be mistaken for a regular pack of hawks, but as they approach, their true size becomes clear. The dark brown birds are larger in person than I'd ever imagined. They're actually somewhere in the range of a smaller single-pilot plane. Their yellow talons stretch beneath them and their beaks snap at the air, ready to feed. The rocs evade the front of the train, veering off to either side. We watch as four of them fly past, make a banking turn in perfect formation and approach the outer walls of the third car. Then, they dig their talons into the glass.

The passengers unfortunate enough to be in the last car, where we were only minutes earlier, scream out as glass showers down on them. They surge forward, climbing on top of one another, but the train cars are so packed that the passengers can barely move. Before any of them makes any headway, the transparent joint between cars 2 and 3 tears and the third car is ripped from the back of the train. It falls away to a symphony of screams from those on board. The rocs, their talons still imbedded in the glass, guide it towards the red rocks below.

"Holy shit," says Mr. Zeckel, breaking his own rule. A bunch of the students in our class are pushing forward now, trying to stay away from the back of the train which just got a hell of a lot closer. Two more rocs are circling now, eying the students closest to the edge.

"We're almost out of here!" yells the conductor. I look forward, peeling my eyes off the horror behind us, to see that we are fast approaching another security gate. But as I look back, I realize it won't come soon enough. The birds fly level to the train and extend their clawed talons to grab two guys from our theater club who are doing their best to swat the birds away. Everyone is crying or screaming or some mixture of the two. One bird nips at the girl who had the violin solo in our commercial, and though the roc doesn't take her, it leaves a bleeding gash in her arm.

"Hold this," says Mr. Zeckel, handing me his oversized backpack. He practically shoves it into my arms before crawling up onto where the seat backs meet in the middle of the train car.

"Mr. Zeckel!" I cry.

"I'm not going to be the type of teacher that sits back and watches an eagle eat my students!" he proclaims fiercely, because that is apparently a 'type' of teacher you can be. He moves quickly towards the end of the train. One of the rocs reaches out and digs its talons into Andrew Felders' leg. *No! Not hot set design guy!* Felders reaches out for his friends who grab hold of him. They pull, but the roc pulls harder. It's like a sick game of tug of war.

"Don't let go!" he yells, and I figure he's about to slip when Mr. Zeckel actually lunges out of the back of the train car, wrapping his arms around the eagle's neck in a choke hold. The bird squawks angrily as they fall out of sight together. Felders gets pulled back onto the train, but his leg looks . . . really bad. Too bad to describe.

"Mr. Zeckel!" yells Erika, who hasn't stopped crying this whole time.

"Brace for impact!" yells the conductor. We all hold on once more as the now two-car train bursts through two more gates and emerges outside the dome. Beneath us, the rocky landscape clears and is quickly replaced by lush forest.

"We're going too fast to make this turn!" yells the conductor.

At a speed that is faster than I've ever seen even a normal train go, we take the sharp right turn. Everyone spills to the left as the train leans into the turn. There's a sound beneath us like the scraping of metal on metal. I spot a shower of sparks shooting off from the train through the glass nearest to me.

Car 2 is the next to go. Under the pressure of the turn, the glass between it and the adjoining car shatters and then, the whole car tips. The joints rip and detach from the front car. Car 2, and most of our fellow students, falls away and disappears beneath the canopy of leaves with a thunderous crash and a cacophony of screams.

Our car goes next, leaning until it falls off the tracks. The train car spins in midair. We all ricochet off the wall, then the ceiling, then the opposite wall. Left is up, and right is down. I lose all sense of direction. Pain shoots through my limbs as I collide with the walls, the seats, other students, and Mr. Zeckel's bag, which is hurled around alongside us. I look up to see the roof rushing towards me and then I slam head first into it.

Like turning off a television, the world closes in around me, and everything goes black.

I wake up lying on my back. At least I think I'm on my back. The world is super fuzzy. As I turn my head the world around me just looks like this bright blob of light. Every bone in my body hurts. Especially my left hand. My throbbing, broken hand. I place my right arm, bent at the elbow, to my side and roll onto it so that I can push myself into a sitting position. The ground under my hand loosens and I see thick mud seeping around my fingers.

"Ugh." Now that I'm sitting up, I try to shake my hand to get some of the mud off, but it's a futile effort because my clothes and hair are covered in the brown muck and nothing short of three showers, a bath and standing in front of a fire hose is going to have any effect now.

I look around as my vision starts to focus and things that I initially saw in triple, become single. *Erika, Zach, anyone.* My fragmented thoughts piece together as I try not to assume the worst. Surely I'm not the only person to have survived the crash. Every muscle in my body objects as I turn to take in my surroundings.

The train car looks as though it's been in a fight with a much bigger, meaner train car. The glass walls are entirely smashed, and the chassis is bent and broken. It lies in a giant heap to my left. To my right is a large pool of water with thick green moss and lily pads floating along its surface. There are several similar pools around me, making it seem as though we've crashed into some sort of swamp. The air is sticky. Flies land on me, rub their front legs together eagerly and take off. I don't blame them. I'm pretty much at my most disgusting right in this moment.

"Erika?" I call out. "Noah? Zach?" I roll my eyes at the prospect of being left alive with only Zach. That would be my luck.

"Guhhh," I hear a deep male voice groan from the direction of the water on my right. I slowly stand up. My legs are aching something fierce but I'm pretty sure I can walk. I take a few stiff steps in the direction of the voice, and then fall back to the ground on my knees. The impact splashes some of the grime onto my face. I spit a few times, desperate to get the taste of mud out of my mouth. I've had a bad enough day without having to eat mud. I lift myself off the ground, and this time my feet find some much needed stability.

I move slowly, searching for signs of the voice,

keeping an eye out for any creatures that might call this place home. I don't know where in the park we are at this point, and so far, I'm two for two on mythical creatures trying to eat me so I don't want to take any chances.

As I near the pond, I catch a glimpse of purple fabric between the branches of a large bush. I make my way to it and find the train conductor sprawled on the ground, clutching his side with both hands.

"Sir?" My voice is scratchy like my throat might be layered with dust. "You okay?"

"I . . . I can't . . . get up."

I lean down and help him sit up. He groans in pain but manages to help me lift him into a seated position.

"T-thank you," he says. He takes a few deep breaths and then looks at me. "Gerard Huff," he wheezes, slightly out of breath. "That's my name. Figure you ought to know it in case . . ." he trails off.

"Henry," I say. "Henry Lau."

"Thank you, Henry," he says. He pulls a purple-spotted white handkerchief from the breast pocket of his uniform and wipes his forehead with it. At this point though, he's just displacing the dirt rather than removing it. "We ought to take a look around, get our bearings. If we can find the train line, we can follow it to one of the stations and call back to Command. Though I'm sure they'll be sending out patrols to look for us. Then again . . ." He coughs into his handkerchief.

"Then again?" I ask.

"A security message came over the comms system before everything went awry," he says. "Park-wide power failures. Seemed like everything was shutting down. Communications cut off right before the Kraken attacked the train."

"So, what does that mean?" I ask.

He sighs but doesn't respond right away.

"Are you saying," I gulp. "They might not be coming for us?"

"I shouldn't be telling you any of this. Protocols are pretty strict, you know? Wouldn't want to panic you."

"Just tell me," I snap. "I'd rather be panicked than oblivious."

He takes a staggered breath. "They might not know where everyone is. I'm fairly certain they don't. Not yet anyway." He coughs again, and I can't help but notice the red specks of blood in the handkerchief when he pulls it away from his mouth.

"Okay," I say. "Okay." I say it again, because honestly, I'm just trying to process all of this. I mean, we just survived a train crash, not to mention being attacked by a handful of mythical creatures. Our teacher is probably dead. That alone makes me feel nauseous. Whatever happens today, however this ends we're going to be part of something that makes the world news. We'll probably be questioned by police and reporters about what happened here. A park that claims to be the safest theme park on Earth is experiencing, potentially, a park-wide power outage coupled with multiple deaths and even more injuries. This is already a huge deal and it's nowhere near over. *Erika. Zach. Noah. All our classmates. All those people.* God, I hope they're all okay. Even Zach.

I squeeze my eyes closed and swallow down the fear in my throat because what other choice do I have? I'm not about to lose my shit in the middle of this swamp with this guy possibly dying in front of me. When I open my eyes, I turn my head, looking for any sort of clue as to what direction we should be heading first. I don't even know if Gerard can move, let alone walk. But we've got to try because the alternative is to leave him here in the mud.

My eyes scan the ground and the swamp, and suddenly I feel a cold chill run down my spine. As I'm looking at the surface of the swamp, I notice two big round eyes looking back at me from just above the water's surface.

I gasp, falling backwards into the mud. The creature looks almost human except that its skin is wrinkly and

101

green the way you might expect a very old witch to look. It has a spherical depression in the top of its head, almost like a bowl, which holds a small bit of water. Long black wisps of hair grow around the head-bowl, matting along the creature's face and neck and finally disappearing into the water.

"H-hello?" I try to be respectful because as scary as this thing looks, I don't want to just assume it's pure evil and provoke it. Then again, I've a pretty good guess of what it is, and from everything I've read, I know that this thing isn't about to jump out of the swamp and give us a friendly hug.

"What is it?" asks Gerard, who hasn't seen the creature yet.

"Um, nothing," I try to sound reassuring. Instead I just sound like I'm lying. I'm a pretty terrible liar and I don't see why this moment would change that.

The creature lifts its head to reveal the rest of its face which is dripping black water. Its mouth is pointed like a beak and covered with deep wrinkles that would take a human being years of chain-smoking to obtain. The turtle-like shell on the creature's back verifies my worst fears: we're sitting smack dab in the middle of Kappa Country.

Kappa lore originated in Japan. Stories vary but none of them are good. At worst, this creature likes to remove human organs from a person's butt. I wish I was kidding. At best they like to sumo wrestle. Stories also say they like cucumbers, but since I don't usually carry one around, distracting it with one is out of the question. Besides, I don't see Gerard making a quick getaway anytime soon. The kappa lifts a slimy, reptilian arm and smacks its webbed hand into the mud on the bank of the swamp.

"Okay, we need to move," I say, positioning myself behind Gerard and wrapping my arms under his armpits so that I might be able to drag him backwards.

"I thought you said it was nothing," he says, fear creeping into his voice.

"I lied, Gerard!" I yell. The creature lifts its other arm and slaps a second hand into the mud. I pull on Gerard, pushing my feet deep into the mud for leverage. It takes all my strength to move just a few inches, but at the rate the kappa is moving, if I can get a steady pace going, we might just have a chance at surviving this.

The kappa opens its mouth and lets out a sound like a toad croaking. Suddenly, a long black tongue shoots out of its mouth, crosses the space between us, and wraps itself around Gerard's left leg.

"It's got me!" Gerard yells.

"I can see that!" I pull on Gerard with every muscle in my body. The kappa's got more strength in that tongue than I've got left in my whole body. I can feel it pulling us in. My feet dig deeper into the mud as we slide steadily towards the swamp. Gerard is clawing, trying to get a grip on the ground, but the mud is slick, and he can't seem to stop our sliding any more than I can. I pull desperately on his arms. I feel like I'm more likely to dislocate one than to actually save this guy, but I can't just give up and let him be eaten by this Teenage Mutant Ninja Turtle reject.

"Help me!" he yells, because apparently that's not what I've *been* doing. "Please! Help me!"

Pulling against the kappa is no use. We're sliding closer and closer and I'm out of strength. My muscles, or lack thereof, are too worn out to be of any use. My broken hand is swollen to all hell. I'm not going to save this guy doing what I've been doing. I think back to my Google search on kappa's when I was reading about all the creatures that Mythos was breeding. Okay, so cucumbers are out, but there has to be something else. My eyes dart to the bowl embedded in the top of the kappa's head, and a memory comes back to me like a jolt of electricity. Supposedly, if even a little water should fall from the kappa's head dish, they'll be severely weakened. Okay, easier said than done. Maybe that works in a fairy tale, but in real life this thing is horrifying and I'm not about to run up and poke it just to knock some water off its head. Then again . . .

An idea strikes me, and I don't give myself enough time to second guess how incredibly stupid what I'm about to do is. I lay Gerard down, which he isn't at all happy about.

"Don't leave me!" he yells as he slides towards the waiting kappa even faster than before.

"I'm not," I say, running around him. "Just trust me." In an effort to not give the kappa any time to deduce my stupid plan, I move quickly, grabbing the kappa's tongue with both my hands and giving it a hearty yank. The kappa's head whips forward as nearly half the water resting in the dish atop its head spills out onto the muddy ground. The fallen water sizzles smoke as it hits the mud.

The kappa instantly retracts its tongue, hisses at me like a pissed off cat, and then dives back into the murky swamp.

I'm not gonna lie. I'm pretty damn proud of myself.

"Yes!" I yell, and I actually punch my fists into the air. Maybe this is what athletes feel like when they score a goal. I don't want to progress any stereotype that gay guys can't play sports because it's not true, but even when I was a little kid, long before my sexuality became part of the picture, I knew that sports was not going to play any sort of role in my life. That being said, Dad was always a big college football fan, and while I never wanted to play, sitting beside him on the sofa and watching the game every Sunday has always sort of been our thing.

"Did you see that?" I ask Gerard who's literally panting and heaving as he tries to catch his breath. His belly lifts and falls as his lungs desperately grab onto any air they can find. "Come on Gerard. We did it! We survived. We've totally got this. You can relax now." What I don't see are the five kappas behind me all emerging from the swamp, all eyes fixed on me, all head bowls full and ready for a fight. They move together, rising out of the water and converging on me. Gerard's eyes go wide as their mouths open and their tongues launch towards me. Just as they're about to wrap themselves around me, two arms wrap snuggly around my waist and pull me haphazardly to safety. Gerard isn't so lucky.

As my savior and I slam into the ground, I watch the kappa tongues grab Gerard by his arms, legs and neck. They drag him screaming across the muddy ground. Within seconds, he's pulled into the water and disappears along with the kappas beneath the surface. A few bubbles break the surface and then the water settles; still and flat, like a pane of glass.

I gasp in horror. This isn't how this is supposed to go. I just *saved* Gerard. I just used my brain and came up with a badass way to defeat the kappa and now we should be celebrating. But that's not what happened. What really happened was that I got cocky which almost got me killed. I feel an immense swell of shame forming in the pit of my stomach because when his family wakes up tomorrow, they will be short a Gerard, and it's my fault. I've never felt more horrible than I do right now.

I have this theory, and I know it sounds really shitty, but hear me out. I believe that people are born inherently bad and they have to work really hard to be good. In a weird way, it makes me feel better about the current state of the world. Like, people can't help treating each other like crap. They were born that way. I like to think that I'm one of the good ones. That I work extra hard every day to go against my natural instincts and actually make the world a better place. But today I failed. Today I cheered myself for a job half done, and someone died because of it.

"You're okay," says my rescuer, the only reason I'm not at the bottom of the swamp being eaten alive by kappas instead of Gerard. "You're okay. Just breathe." Only now do I notice that I'm gasping for air. Only now do I notice that I stopped breathing while I watched Gerard go under and my lungs are begging me to give them back some control. Tears are streaming down my face uncontrollably. I'm in shock. "You're okay. You're okay."

I look up to see who's holding me, and I'm surprised to find myself looking into Noah's eyes. *Noah*. My creepy stalker, Noah. Noah and his green eyes in all their glory. I do my best to pull myself together as quickly as I can and stand up, freeing myself from his hold because quite honestly, I've had enough of this guy today. Hell, I've had enough of him to last a lifetime. What's his deal? On the ship. On the train. Here. He just keeps being *here*. I'm just not in the mood for his overprotective alpha male bullshit or his green eyes that never seem to look away or his carefree attitude.

An image of Vincent pops into my head. Sweet, kind, vulnerable Vincent. I'm suddenly glad he wasn't on the train because it means he's somewhere safe. It means he's waiting for me, probably worried sick. Speaking of worried sick . . .

"Have you seen Erika?" I ask. "Is she okay?"

"She's fine. Or as fine as any of us at this point."

I sigh with relief. I dust myself off, shaking my hands to get off some of the mud. I immediately regret it because my hand hasn't gotten any less broken and it hurts like hell to move, let alone shake. I grab it reflexively, inhaling sharply.

"Let me see," says Noah, stepping towards me. He

steps into my bubble and I instinctively step back. I don't care for being that close to people I barely know. Especially to people who can barely be bothered to take out their earphones long enough to talk to me.

"I'm fine," I say.

"I found Mr. Zeckel's bag," he says. "Maybe he's got some pain killers or something."

"I said I'm fine."

"Okay tough guy, whatever you say." He stomps past me. "Maybe you can 'be fine' while we walk. We shouldn't be around when those things decide they want some dessert."

He picks up a big backpack off the ground. It's seen better days, but I recognize it as Mr. Zeckel's. He digs in it, pulls out a little white bottle and tosses it to me. I don't catch it, but I feel it graze my right hand before it plops down in the mud. That's basically the same as catching it, right? Since the day I was born, I've never been much good at catching things. It's like some crazy character flaw. The world could be ending and all I have to do is catch something to save it and I can guarantee you we would all die. I lean down and pick it up to see that it's a bottle of extra strength Tylenol.

"Better than nothing," says Noah. "You'll have to swallow it dry." He chuckles.

"What's so funny?" I ask.

"In a less shitty place, that would have been an excellent moment for a 'That's what he said.'"

"Wow," I say, and I hate myself because despite how much this guy pisses me off, I can't help but smile. "Real mature."

"Listen. I used to have a pretty strict no 'that's-what-they-said' jokes policy, but my ex ..." he trails off and I see the smile fade from his face as something flickers across his eyes. "He taught me to appreciate them."

He? Did Noah just say *he?* Is there mud in my ears? Up until now I've been pretty certain that I'm the only gay kid in my class. Well, me and Vincent that is. But now new-kid Noah just admitted openly to having an ex who is a *he.* Is anyone else hearing this? Did I hit my head in the train crash and get a concussion? Maybe I died in the train crash and this is all some sort of weird after life. But then again, if it's real ...

What am I even thinking here? I don't like Noah. I'm actually sort of creeped out by Noah. I can't just start liking him because he likes guys. That's all kinds of desperate, not to mention a betrayal of my own self-worth. This guy has treated me and Erika like shit since the moment he saw us. The fact that he's gay or bi or whatever doesn't excuse the fact that he's a giant asshole. So, I wipe the smile off my face and follow after him.

"You're right," I say. "It's a joke for a less shitty place." I open the pill bottle, take out four Tylenol (because I've got a broken hand and two simply won't do) and toss them down my throat. I swallow them dry, which is about as awful as it sounds, joke or not. Then I hand the bottle back to Noah.

"Thanks."

He nods and secures the bottle back in the bag before tossing the bag over his shoulder. "Everyone else is waiting for us on a hill not too far from here," he says. "I volunteered to come out and find you hoping you'd be near the wreckage. The rest of us got thrown pretty far."

"Why?" I ask. Normally it's a question I would ask in my head, but despite it being only midday, I'm exhausted, and my filter has basically given up.

"Erika threw up a couple times after the crash. Figured she could use the time to rest. That Janice girl is probably useless on a normal day, let alone a life or death one. Zach was trying to get her to calm down and I'm pretty sure the other guy, Thomas he said his name was, would just get himself lost rather than actually find you."

"Ugh, Thomas is with you guys?" I know this sounds like a pretty shitty thing to say but trust me, if you knew Thomas Ruiz, you'd say it too. On the other hand, I feel a

111

weight lift off me I didn't even realize was there. Erika *and* Zach are safe. That alone makes everything a little less awful.

"Seems like there are a lot of cliffs around here though. I'm sure if he talks too much, we can always push him off one."

I almost laugh. God dammit. Noah almost got me to laugh. But I manage to catch myself and just do a cool guy eye roll. That's right. Bask in how much I don't think you're sort of charming and how much I don't like your drop-dead gorgeous eyes. Suck on that. I mean, don't suck on it because . . . crap, now I'm thinking about *that* of all things.

"Lead the way," I say in hopes that this will give Noah a reason to turn around and not see how red I'm turning.

My plan works. Noah turns and heads off into the underbrush, crumpling the ferns and shrubbery as he goes. I follow close behind in the path he's created, taking in the wilderness around us. Thin shafts of light break through the canopy of tree branches overhead, illuminating the path and the vegetation that grows from the wet ground. Large trees covered in moss and thick vines stand guard, and every now and then a bright blue orchid is visible, permeating the overwhelming greenery. The flowers seem to glow ever so slightly, but it could be my thoroughly jostled head playing tricks on me.

The train car fades into the distance behind us. How any of us survived the crash, I'll never know, but I'm happy to be leaving it behind. Though something tells me the memory of the crash and Gerard's death will haunt me for the rest of my life.

A thought occurs to me, and I reach into my pocket to pull out my cell phone. Unsurprisingly, my screen is black and cracked to all hell. "Anyone manage to get any cell service?" I ask hopefully.

"Nope," says Noah. "Everyone's phone is either broken or lost. Janice's survived the crash, but she's got no service out here, and she turned it off to conserve battery."

"Damn," is all I can say. It figures that the one time we need our phones for something other than checking statuses or uploading our selfies, they're completely worthless. I stare down at my busted screen in silence. I really liked this phone. We snake our way up an inclined path as the world around us steadily grows brighter.

Erika sees me before I see her. "Henry!" she yells. I look up towards the hill's crest where the others are waiting. They've managed to find a clearing in this forest, and I can actually see a blue sky behind them. She runs to me and wraps her arms around me, and I swear to God it's the tightest hug I've ever gotten from anyone. I hug her back because I'm just as happy to see her alive as she is to see me. Erika is like my sister. If I'd lost her, I don't know what I'd do. "Thank God you're safe," she whispers in my ear.

"You too," I say. I'm crying again. When we finally let go of each other, I follow her and Noah up to stand with the others. Zach nods at me because that's how bros say hi. Janice lifts her hand in a slight wave and Thomas gives me this weird two finger salute.

"Alright there, Henry?" he asks.

"Broken hand and you're here," I say smartly. "But yeah, I'm okay."

"Good to hear!" he exclaims, not catching on to my sarcasm. "I was just saying that we need to figure out a plan. Now that we found a good clear spot, they should be able to find us when they do a fly over. Still, it wouldn't hurt to start a bonfire or spell out SOS with coconuts."

"There might not be a fly over," I say gloomily, remembering Gerard's words. "They might not even know we're this far out here. Not yet anyway."

"Why the hell not?" asks Zach.

"Gerard, the train conductor, he said that before everything went to hell, he was getting alerts about a park-wide power outage. There's even a chance they're in worse shape than we are."

"Well where's this Gerard guy now?" asks Thomas. "Maybe he knows somewhere safe we could go?"

"He's dead," I say.

"Oh," says Thomas in a whisper.

"Maybe we could find somewhere safe to wait for things to calm down," says Janice.

"That's not a bad idea," says Erika. "I'm sure they've got facilities out here. Think about it. What if one of the park rangers or technicians gets a flat tire. They've got to have somewhere they can go that's not all the way back in Town Square."

"It's a good idea," I say. "But if the power really is down park wide . . ."

"Then so are electrical fences, mechanized locks, landlines. The list goes on and on," says Noah, stealing my thunder.

"Exactly," I add. "The animals won't have anything keeping them contained. At least not until the power is restored. Which means that nowhere out here is safe right now."

"Shit," says Zach. Janice leans into him, burying her face in his chest. "You're telling me they didn't plan for a power outage like this when they built the fences? Isn't this park supposed to be state of the art? Haven't they seen

115

Jurassic Park or one of its nineteen sequels?"

"That's the thing," I say. "The power doesn't just go out park-wide on Mythos. There are contingencies upon contingencies. A park-wide power outage isn't just bad, it's impossible, unless . . .

"Unless?" asks Erika.

"Unless this wasn't an accident. A guy like Dawson Saks doesn't create something like this place without making a few enemies along the way."

Everyone goes silent.

"Well that's super shitty for him," says Noah. "But our problems are a lot simpler than dealing with crazy corporate espionage. We just have to survive. So that leaves one option." He steps up to the edge of the hilltop we're on and looks out over the landscape. For the first time, I realize that we must be pretty high up because we can see a lot of the park from here. Far in the distance we can just barely make out the top of the highest spire on the Grand Palace. "We have to get there." He points to the lone spire, its flag waving gently in the breeze.

"You're insane," says Thomas. "We'll never make it."

"If we stay out here, we're as good as dead," I say. "It's our only chance. Maybe the power will come back and then we can change course and find somewhere to wait for rescue, but until then, all we can really do is head for the one place we know is safe."

"Alright," says Erika. "I'm in."

I look at her in surprise because I guess I didn't expect her to be the first person on board with this.

"What?" she asks. "Don't think that just because I'm a diva that I'm not willing to trek through the wilds to stay alive. We're in this now. No amount of whining is going to change that." Have I mentioned that I love her?

"I don't wanna go!" whines Janice.

Erika raises her eyebrows in Janice's direction.

"It's our only option," says Zach. "I'm in."

"Me too," says Thomas.

"I'm out," says Noah. We all look at him, bewildered. A sly grin dances across his face. "Just kidding."

We all turn to look out over the park, out over the journey we're about to take. I want to say that there's a swell of majestic music playing at our backs as we get ready to undertake the task of finding our way back to the Palace—of finding our way back home—but there's no music or fanfare. We're about to head out into the wilds of Mythos Isle and the animals are all running free. We don't get a soaring musical send off. We'll be lucky if we get an obituary.

SEVEN

"So, we've had hate-eagles and monster-squid. You guys saw swamp-thing. Any idea what other freaks of nature we'll be meeting on our island tour?" asks Erika. She's putting on a brave face, faking her way through this horrible situation via the magic of sarcasm. But I know her too well. Deep down she's freaking out. We all are.

"You think those were bad? Let me tell you, our tour is just getting started. We've still got all sorts of hungry critters left to see," I say. I'm not really in the mood to talk, but the silence is far worse than the noise. It doesn't help that every time I close my eyes, I see Mr. Zeckel jumping out of the train or Gerard being dragged into the water or the two men disappearing with the train's last car into the mouth of the Kraken.

"Oh goodie!" quips Erika. "I hope something likes to eat eyeballs. I've about had it with these old things."

We both giggle like a pair of old ladies who live in Downton Abbey.

"It's not funny you guys!" snaps Janice, who's already

angry that Zach won't hold her hand since walking hand-in-hand isn't really conducive to trekking down a hill with dense vegetation. The sun has disappeared behind the trees and I'm trying to ignore the fact that it's getting further across the sky by the second. Pretty soon it will start to lower behind the horizon. The day has been awful enough. I dread what new horrors will find us in the night.

"Calm down Janice," says Erika. "We're just trying to make the best out of a bad situation."

"Well it's upsetting me, so can you please just stop?" she requests, but she says it in such a way that it sounds more like an order.

"Oh, I'm so sorry your royal highness," mocks Erika. "Pardon me if I don't cater to your every whim. Not that you can do anything about it. Last I checked, your posse isn't here to write threatening messages on my locker in red lipstick if I don't behave. Guess you'll just have to put up with the commoners for once. You know, the way everyone at school puts up with you."

"When my father finds out about this—" Janice starts, her face turning red.

"He'll what?" asks Erika. Any pretense of joking or teasing has left her voice. "Cheat on your mom with his secretary again?"

"Erika!" Zach shouts. "That's enough!"

No one comes to Erika's rescue. Not this time. We all know she's gone too far. It's a secret that Janice's parents almost got divorced last year because her Dad cheated, so naturally the whole school knows about it. They ended up going to therapy and even stayed together in the end. But once something like that gets out, everyone only talks about the bad parts. I really dislike Janice, but I sort of admire her for dealing with all of that and still showing up to school with a smile on her face. I even get why she's such a terror at school. In the end, we're all just like the animals out here. We all have our quirks. We all dislike people messing with our pack, and we all have defense mechanisms. Hers just happens to be acting like a total bitch.

"Whatever," says Erika as she pushes past me and storms off by herself.

I watch her walk away and my heart breaks a little bit. Yeah, what Erika said was cold-hearted, but let's face it, Janice has been a bully to Erika ever since Middle School.

"Yikes," says Thomas. "Time of the month, huh?"

"Seriously?!" I snap, rounding on Thomas because the last thing I need right now is Thomas making incredibly sexist comments. I have never wished so hard for someone I know to get eaten by a dragon as I do right now.

"What?" he asks, because he actually can't see the lack of tact in his comment.

"Thomas, right?" asks Noah, stepping between me and Thomas. Maybe he thinks he's breaking up a fight before it happens. But no matter how angry I am, I don't think I'd ever throw the first punch or even the second. I'm just not a fighter. I like to think it's because I believe peace and love is the best course, but I think deep down I don't fight because I know I would lose. And like I said, I'm a rule follower and fighting is, in pretty much every rulebook, against the rules.

"Yeah, that's right," says Thomas, puffing out his chest.

"Cool," says Noah. "Look, I just wanted to take a moment to tell you that you're actually the worst. Like, truly awful. I'd just hate for you to go through life without someone letting you know. It's sort of like letting someone walk outside with their shirt inside out. It's rude, you know?"

Woah. We've all stopped to look at Noah and Thomas because, as they say in the old west, them is fightin' words.

"What did you just say to me?" asks Thomas.

"I said: you're the wor—"

"Guys!" Erika's voice echoes through the trees and

we all turn in the direction she disappeared to.

"Erika?" I say into the darkness, taking off into the trees at a run. I could easily be running right into the open mouth of a dragon or some other terrible creature, but if Erika's in danger, I could care less. I burst through a large bush to find her standing safely with her eyes fixed forward. I let out a sigh of relief because from what I can tell at least she's not hurt.

"Jesus, you scared the hell out of me," I say.

"Look," she says, pointing down the hill.

I turn to see, well, I can't quite explain it. It's a building. That much is certain. The forest has literally grown over it, covering it in vines and dirt so that you actually have to look fairly closely to see it. It seems totally out of place. It's built out of cement and might have been some sort of security facility. It's not very tall or flashy, and it looks as though it hasn't been used or even thought about for years. There are a few long windows along the sides of the building, but they're clouded over with a thick layer of grime.

Down the hill from us is a set of double doors inlaid into what I would assume is the front of the building because there's a rough dirt path leading up to it. Above the doors lies a faded message. The engraved words read: Mythos (and on the next line) Powered by Belief. It's weird because even the word 'Mythos' isn't in its signature font. It's like finding one of those truck-stop stores that sells copycat off-brand Disney souvenirs.

"What is this place?" asks Erika, breaking the silence.

"I . . . have no idea," I say.

"Well that's concerning," she mutters. "You know everything about Mythos. If you don't have an entry on this in your brain, then it can't be good."

"Maybe it's just an old facility that they replaced later on," I say, trying to sound optimistic.

"Or maybe they left it out here in hopes that no one would find it," she says ominously.

"You guys okay?" asks Zach coming up behind us with his new accessory (Janice) wrapped around his arm. I hear Janices are all the rage in French couture fashion.

"What is that?" asks Thomas, coming up behind them.

"Something you only see on the behind the scenes tour," adds Noah. "The behind the behind the scenes tour."

"Looks pretty secure," I say optimistically. "Maybe there's a landline or something in there."

"I thought the power was out," says Zach.

"Sure, but sometimes bunkers like this have landline phones that work during power outages. Or maybe there's a satellite phone or an old two-way radio or something with a generator." I don't actually know what I'm talking about, but something is calling me to this place, and I can't just turn and walk away.

"I'm willing to check it out if you all are," says Thomas. Like we need his approval. I think we'd all gladly leave him outside. "Besides, it's getting dark. We should find some shelter."

"I'd go but I wouldn't want my lady-business to contaminate the place," quips Erika.

Noah lets out a laugh even though Thomas looks mortified. "Look," says Thomas. "I'm sorry, I didn't mean to—"

Erika moves up to Thomas like a viper rounding on their prey. "A woman's emotional state is not governed solely by her period. If you ever make another joke like that, I will kick you in your baby-makers. Do you understand?"

Thomas gulps and nods vigorously.

Noah starts down the hill. "On this episode of Strange Days at Mythos High, Erika teaches Thomas the value of friendship and not being an asshole."

"I'll kick your ass too," she says.

"Fine, but let's do it in there," says Noah, pointing and beginning the descent to the compound. "I'd prefer to call for help before it gets dark. You're all dramatic enough in the daylight. I'd hate to have to see how much drama you all stir up when the lights go out."

Erika looks at me with a bewildered expression, but I just shrug because he's actually right about this. We need to focus on getting back to civilization and not losing our shit on each other. I follow behind him and the others trail after me.

We get to the door and Noah caresses the steel. He stops at the gap between the two doors and slides the tips of his fingers inside, standing to one side. "Help me with this," he says. I step up and place the fingers of my right hand in the crack. My left hand is pretty much useless at this point, but the Tylenol has surprisingly helped some, numbing the torrential pain to a survivable ache. Zach and Erika step up to help us. Janice stands back, hugging herself like she might literally fall to pieces if she doesn't.

"On three," says Noah. "One, two, three." We all pull, putting our weight into hefting the door open. There's a loud groan as the doors slide open on either side. Dust pours down on us from above and I sneeze as some of it invades my nostrils. Dust in my nose and mud in my mouth. This day just keeps getting better and better.

With the door fully open, we step back and look in, though we can't see much. It's pitch-black inside.

"Well this looks like a great place for us all to die horrible deaths," says Noah.

"Truth," says Erika, who isn't quite ready to start making morbid jokes again but doesn't mind seconding one.

Noah pulls Mr. Zeckel's bag off his back and digs around in the front pocket, fishing out a small red Zippo type lighter. "This should help," he says.

"Why does Mr. Zeckel have a lighter?" I ask.

"To use with these, I assume." He pulls out a crumpled pack of cigarettes.

"He taught the anti-drug assembly at school," says Erika, shaking her head. "Hypocrite."

"His bad habit is our good fortune though," says Noah, shouldering the pack again before holding up the lighter and flicking his thumb over it. A small flame bounds to life, just barely illuminating the wide hallway before us. "We'll have to stay close."

"Luckily, we all like each other," says Thomas. He looks around, clearly hoping for a laugh or two but gets nothing from us.

"Whatever," says Zach. "Let's just find a phone and get the hell out of here."

"I'm cold," says Janice. Zach goes to her like a dog on a leash and wraps his arms around her. I can't recall a time where I've ever seen someone become so whipped so fast.

With Noah in the lead, we head into the facility and I can't help hoping that this won't end up being our final resting place. We stick close together, huddling around the flame's light. This first wide hallway stretches down towards another set of double doors. The walls are bare, and cobwebs hang from the ceiling. The doors open after a few shoves, wrenching them free of the rust holding them in place. Past them, we're greeted by what I can only assume is a large room because we can't see the walls or the ceiling.

"Over here," says Zach. He walks to the right of the door we've just come through towards a row of grey cabinets. The first two yield nothing but lab coats and general storage but the third is another story. He pulls it open to reveal several bulky yellow flashlights with handles and large bulbs, all hanging in a row. He pulls them from the cabinet, handing one to each of us. Janice is the first to turn hers on, and I think we're all a little surprised when a bright beam of light bursts from the yellow box, shooting a spotlight onto the ceiling high above.

"How do these still have power?" I ask, turning mine on and panning the beam of light around the huge room. The room itself is filled with white desks littered with papers and folders, long metal counters atop rows of cabinets and drawers, and black desk chairs, most of which have toppled over and lay discarded on the tiled linoleum floor. There's also a fair amount of test tubes, beakers and lab equipment scattered about as well as several large pieces of machinery with long robotic arms which hang limply over abandoned work stations. The whole thing sends chills down my spine.

"This building is most likely connected to the park-wide grid," says Zach. "I assume they've just been sitting here charging. Until the power went out that is." Zach looks at me, taking the last flashlight for himself and turning it on.

We make our way into the middle of the room, the six of us illuminating the large space with six beams of light. Watching the beams move and the spotlights weave around the room, I feel like we're at a concert and someone's turned off the music, not to mention the fun.

"Anyone else notice that this place is sort of a mess?" asks Noah.

"Maybe the scientists didn't like to clean up after themselves," says Janice.

"Yeah," says Noah. "Maybe. But it sort of looks like they left in a hurry."

He's right. Test tubes and files lay everywhere.

Equipment isn't stored properly. Jars of liquid are spilled across countertops and the floor. Regardless of whether or not the scientists who worked here were sticklers for cleanliness, I can't imagine anyone leaving this mess by choice.

"Maybe this is why they left," says Erika. Off to the side of the room, her flashlight is pointed at a hole in the wall where it looks like a bomb has gone off. Bent metal protrudes into the room through the hole. On the other side of the wall is a long hallway which fades to black so that we can't see the end, even with our flashlights pointed down it. "Guess the dragons didn't like being cooped up."

"What makes you think it was a dragon?" I ask.

"Look at the burn marks," she says, moving her light over the edges of the hole. Black residue scars the jagged metal, not to mention the floor under our feet.

"If fire caused this, then it's definitely not a dragon," I say. "Dragons don't breathe fire. Not on Mythos anyway. The geneticists thought it would be too dangerous. Or at least that's the official statement they gave."

"And unofficially?" asks Erika.

"Unofficially, rumors are that they just couldn't get it right."

"Seriously?" asks Erika.

"Maybe they were ashamed of it," I say. "They made

all this happen. This whole park. But despite that, they just couldn't find a way to make a living animal spit fire out of its mouth. If I were them, I'd want it blamed on safety concerns too. An unauthorized biography claims it as Saks' biggest regret in life."

"Men and their pride," says Erika with a grin. "My biggest regret in life is making out with Eric Weavers at Homecoming last year."

I laugh. "Eric Weavers is hot."

"His breath smelled like pickles," she says with a disgusted look on her face.

"Yikes," I concede.

"Well, dragon or not, something definitely blew a hole in this wall," she says, still panning the light over it.

"Yeah," I agree. "Something definitely did."

Zach shows up behind us, shining a light down the corridor on the other side of the exploded wall. "Let's just find a phone and get out of here," he says.

We leave the wall behind and follow the rest of the group through another set of double doors on the east side of the room. We find ourselves in a rectangular room with a long paper-covered desk which is placed against a wall made of thick glass. Several chairs sit at the desk and at least two have fallen backwards onto the floor. The glass acts as a window into four separate rooms, each with a wooden chair behind a school desk. From the ceiling of each of these rooms hangs a tight bundle of wires leading down to a small metal contraption which looks like an inverted mixing bowl. Something tells me it was meant to be placed on someone's head, but only a child's head would fit in such a small bowl. I don't know exactly what I'm looking at, but whatever it is sends goosebumps prickling up and down my arms.

Several years ago, Mythos and Dawson Saks were accused of testing on humans in inhumane ways, but no real evidence was ever brought to light. Eventually the charges were dropped. Still, looking at these rooms, I can't help but wonder if the accusations might have been true. This outright looks exactly like what you'd expect of some psychological experimentation room.

"Woah," says Erika. She's turned to look at the wall behind us where the image of a young boy wearing the metal dish on top of his head is painted onto a baby blue wall like a mural. He's smiling happily with his eyes closed, and there are curling wisps of purple and blue emerging from his head which remind me of photos I've seen of the Northern Lights. Beneath his face is the same dated logo from outside. Mythos: Powered by Belief.

"Powered by creepiness is more like it," says Erika. Our flashlights dancing over the mural somehow make it even more haunting.

"What the hell were they doing here?" I ask.

"It doesn't matter," says Zach, pushing onwards into the adjoining room, slamming the next set of doors open as he traipses through it.

Everyone looks at each other in confusion, but I storm after him, shoving my way through the doors into another large lab. This one is easier to see in because a long window lines one wall. Sunlight reflects off a moss-covered rock wall outside the window, flooding the room with a greenish hue.

"What's your problem, Zach?" I shout. Apparently, I'm done pulling punches when it comes to the two of us.

"My problem?" asks Zach, rounding on me and pointing his flashlight right in my face. "My problem is that I don't want to be trapped out here when the sun goes down. My problem is that this place is creepy as hell and I want to leave. My problem is that we need to be focusing on finding a way out of here and not whatever sick experiments they were doing in this place. But you know what my biggest problem is, Henry?"

"No Zach, I don't," I say, raising my voice. "You know why? Because you won't tell me. You'll barely talk to me! You've completely shut me out since I came out. So, what is your biggest problem, Zach? Please, tell me. Is it that your friend being gay somehow diminishes your manhood? Or somehow makes you less likely to get into heaven? Do I disgust you now? Do you hate me?"

"I do hate you!" he yells. "I hate you for lying to me!" We both go silent. The words 'hate' and 'lie' echo off the walls, reverberating in our ears. We both just stare at each other, our lights held to our sides like Anakin and Obi Wan about to have their final showdown.

Neither one of us dares to break the silence, but the silence *is* broken. A low growl enters our ears. I feel my whole body freeze and my eyes grow wide. As if mirroring each other, Zach and I both turn to look at the long window which stretches along the wall beside us.

Only now do I realize that the moss-covered rock outside isn't made of rock or moss at all. We both aim our lights on the glass as a huge reptilian eye opens from within the green. Its black pupil, long and sharp and snake-like, is surrounded by a red and yellow iris like the eye of Sauron. My breath catches in my throat as it scans the room and then looks right at us.

EIGHT

We should totally run, but we don't. We stay perfectly still. Maybe we think that it can't see us if we don't move, which honestly makes no sense since it's looking right at us. If sight could kill, its glare would eviscerate us on the spot.

"Henry," says Zach, taking a very slow step backwards. "What do we do?"

"I-I don't know," I manage to sputter. "Why are you asking me?"

"Because you're the expert on this stuff. Do you think it can get in here?"

"The walls seem pretty thick," I say. "Like a military bunker. Maybe we're safe?"

"Let's just back out of the room slowly. No sudden moves. Then we'll—"

"AAIIEEEE!" Janice enters the room and immediately starts screaming bloody murder.

Maybe the walls are too thick for the beast to hear, but it suddenly moves proving that theory wrong. It uncurls its body, like a snake uncoiling itself, and stands up. Where before there was a solid green shape in the window, I can now see individual body parts. A large head with two thick horns curving up from just above its eyes makes the dragon look like some otherworldly demon. Curved spikes run along the back of its head and down its thick neck. The creature's body is long and muscular with two enormous scaled wings and a long slender tail which sways and flicks from side to side almost like a housecat. The creature is mostly a lime-green color, but the underside of its head, neck and torso are all cream colored and devoid of the menacing spikes which cover the topside of the beast. It moves lithely on its four legs, rounding on the window and us. Every step it takes shakes the ground and sends a small tremor through the tiled floor which vibrates up my calves.

"Shut up Janice!" snaps Zach, but it's no use. She's still freaking out, which I totally get because I'm also freaking out. The problem is that her freak out is way too loud considering the monster standing just outside the building. Erika moves up behind Janice and wraps her arms around the screaming girl, placing her hand over Janice's mouth, which doesn't silence the screams, but diminishes them for the most part.

"Shhh," says Erika, staring up at the dragon who's

peering curiously back through the window at all of us.

"Everyone okay?" asks Thomas, running through the double doors from the experimentation room. He stops dead in his tracks when he sees the dragon. "Holy shit!" he yells and the dragon's whole head flicks to its right, fixing on Thomas. He drops his flashlight, his hands flying up to cover his mouth. The flashlight hits the hard floor and the bulb explodes with a soft but very audible pop.

The dragon opens its mouth, revealing a set of razor-sharp teeth, and lets loose a roar that is deafening. It's as if a hundred lions and Godzilla have all joined an acapella group. We all cover our ears. There's a sudden slamming and the whole room seems to rock. I lose my footing, stumbling backwards. I look up to see that the dragon has just headbutted the window. It rears back and then slams into the window again. The glass remains remarkably intact, but a crack bursts through the cement wall just below the ceiling. Another headbutt and the crack spreads into several more, racing along the walls like the roots of a tree.

"Time to go," says Zach. He reaches down and pulls me up off the ground and together we run for the doors we originally came through. Thomas ducks back through the door as Erika drags Janice backwards. As we reach the door, the wall behind us implodes, pouring chunks of cement and shards of thick glass into the room as the dragon's head plunges through. It shakes its head free of the dust and debris and then turns to look at us, nostrils flaring, as we barrel through the doorway.

We race through the experimentation room, past the muraled wall. The door behind us explodes off its hinges as a bony clawed hand the size of a compact car bursts through it and digs into the floor, leaving four deep gashes in its wake. We plunge through the next set of doors and now we're running back through the first large lab-like room, dodging upturned chairs and spilled liquids. The beams from our flashlights fly around the room in a dazzlingly hectic light show. The wall behind us explodes into the room, bulldozed by the dragon which is keeping a good pace with us despite the many walls and doors in its path.

"Crap!" yells Zach.

"Come on!" Noah, who's leading the group, holds open the large double doors so that we can all pile through. As soon as we charge through, he follows after Zach and me. We run down the entry hall, out one last set of doors, and then we're outside.

Daylight is dwindling, and night is just around the corner. No one turns off their flashlights. We simply dash into the forest with them still beaming spotlights onto the oversized leaves and trees around us. We can still hear the dragon stomping along behind us, destroying the building from the inside out. It roars again, probably searching desperately for our tracks or our scent or whatever means they use to hunt.

A new sound disrupts the symphony of destruction. It sounds like a large propeller, so huge and powerful, that even a slow rotation would cause a massive swelling of wind. Each revolution creating a force of air like a jet engine. I gasp in a breath realizing that what I'm hearing isn't a gigantic propeller, but the sound of enormous flapping wings.

"Lights off," says Noah, clicking off his flashlight. "We don't need to advertise where we are to that thing." Everyone else follows suit. We're still running through the jungle, but we're all doing so in crouched positions, as if the dragon might swoop down on us and carry us off if we stand upright. We follow a path, if you can call it that, down a hill through the brush. Orange and red hues dance along the foliage as the sun begins to set to our right. At least we know we're heading south, which is the right direction if we ever hope to make it back to the Palace.

"There's something up here," calls Thomas who's in the lead.

The overgrowth of trees falls away suddenly as we

come to a cliff overlooking a canyon. I expect there's some sort of river or stream at the bottom, though it could be dried up, but the truth is that we can't even *see* the bottom. A thick fog rolls through the canyon almost like a river of clouds. Anything could be hiding within it. There's no way to know. Dangling in front of us, however, is a long rope and plank bridge which stretches from the side of the canyon we're on all the way to the opposite side with hand railings so severely damaged that they hardly serve a purpose anymore. It looks about as sketchy and ominous as it sounds. It's actually wide enough for a small jeep to cross it, and my guess is that many jeeps *have* crossed it since it looks fairly old and out of commission.

"No," says Janice. "No fucking way." She's shaking her head violently at the sight of the bridge.

As if to challenge her decision, a loud roar calls out behind us. The sound reverberates off the canyon walls, echoing around us in surround sound.

"We have to cross," says Zach. "We have to keep moving south. It's the only way Janice."

"That bridge is a breath away from falling apart," says Janice. "If you make me cross it, I am breaking up with you."

"If we don't cross that bridge, we'll be dead," is Zach's come-back, which is a pretty fair point.

"I think if we all go one at a time and keep a fair distance between ourselves, we should be okay," Thomas informs us. "These old rope bridges are usually sturdier than people give them credit for."

"Oh, you have a lot of experience with old rope bridges?" says Noah dryly.

"As a matter of fact, I do," says Thomas. "I used to build them when I was in the Boy Scouts. Even got a badge in knot-tying for it."

"Super," says Noah. "Was that before or after the rampant homophobia badge?"

"Guys!" yells Erika. "If we're doing this, let's just do it."

"We have to," I say.

"I can't!" yells Janice.

"Just go first," says Zach. "Think about all the movies with bridges like this one. The first person always makes it across, right?"

I can't see how this is a valid argument, but to my surprise Janice actually nods and turns towards the bridge, adding: "Okay. You're right."

"I'll be right behind you," says Zach.

"I'd prefer if Erika followed me," says Janice. "She's lighter."

"She just called you fat," says Noah.

"Harsh," says Erika. "But true. I'll go after Janice."

"Then I'll go," says Thomas. He doesn't provide any reasoning behind it, but no one wants to hear him talk anymore, so no one argues the point.

"I'll go after Thomas," says Zach.

"Then Henry," says Noah. I shoot him a disgruntled look because I can say when I'll be crossing the bridge on my own, thank you very much.

"Fine," I say. "Let's just go." I can hear the trees crashing and toppling behind me as the dragon continues his tour of destruction into the forest. From the sound of it, I would guess that the dragon is diving into the trees, searching for us and then taking off again. We're being hunted. It's not far behind us now, and every second we waste on deciding our marching order brings us that much closer to being a dragon's dinner.

"Okay," says Janice. "Okay, okay, okay." She takes deep breaths as she approaches the bridge. It's anchored to the side of the canyon by thick ropes secured to large iron rods which are plunged deep into the ground. It's not like we're taking a scenic walk here. No one in their right mind would be out here using this bridge as part of some sort of nature hike. The bridge is probably fine to support all of our weight, but no one is willing to take that chance after the day we've had so far.

Janice closes her eyes, feeling for the sickly rope railings at her sides. Then, carefully, she takes her first steps out onto the bridge. "Okay, okay," she continues as she puts one foot in front of the other. Don't get me wrong, I don't like Janice and after this is all over, she and I will go right back to not talking to each other, but in this very moment, I'm actually pretty proud of her. I don't care who you are, conquering your fears is always impressive.

"You got this," says Zach who keeps glancing over his shoulder at the jungle behind us where the sound of trees falling is getting louder by the second.

Janice is several feet out on the bridge when Erika nods and follows after her, carefully stepping onto the wooden planks groaning below her. Even with their creaky complaints, none of the planks actually gives way.

Thomas steps up to the bridge. "Watch and learn boys."

"It's crossing a rope bridge, not pitching the world series," says Zach.

Thomas continues to drone on. "I've always wanted to pitch in the world series but my arms both suffer from weak joints which causes me to—"

"Just go!" All three of us shout at him from behind. Thankfully, Thomas shuts up and continues along the bridge. Janice is about halfway across now, with Erika slowly gaining on her, trying not to go so fast that she rocks the bridge or actually catches up.

Zach follows Thomas and then it's my turn. I take a deep breath and step out onto the wood, feeling the bridge jerk beneath my feet now that four of us are on it. It's definitely an odd feeling. I'm suddenly super aware that I'm no longer standing on solid ground. I also instantly make the mistake of looking down. Through the cracks between the wooden planks I can clearly see the white fog billowing below us. Small wisps curl and split off the main cloud. It's almost as if I'm looking down on heaven. If it weren't for my intense fear of falling into it, I think I would actually find it beautiful.

That thought throws me a little, because it's infinitely strange to notice beauty when you're scared out of your mind and running for your life. I force myself to keep my eyes up and start walking. Not far across, I feel the whole bridge give a little jolt and somehow, I know that Noah has just stepped out onto the first plank.

"I did it!" yells Janice. I can see her on the far side of the canyon with her hands in the air and tears streaming down her face. She's even smiling. I guess even in the worst of circumstances, it's always a little bit fulfilling to achieve something you once thought impossible. I'm watching Janice jump up and down excitedly as I cross the halfway point of the bridge, when something that's been nagging at the back of my mind finally catches up to the front. I haven't heard any roars or trees being crushed in quite some time, which means that the dragon has either given up or—

A deafening roar echoes around us, so loud that the air actually vibrates. To my horror, this one doesn't come from behind us but *next to us*. To my left, the dragon is flying through the canyon, heading straight for us.

"Run!" Everyone throws caution to the wind as they take off towards the far side. Erika reaches it quickly and Thomas isn't far behind. The running causes waves in the bridge, making it even more unstable. A handful of feet away, I see Zach about to get to the end of the bridge when I make the unfortunate mistake of looking back.

The dragon opens its mouth and takes a bite right out of the bridge behind us, just barely missing Noah who lunges forward at the last second, grabbing onto the planks in front of him. The bridge snaps in half. Wood splinters off and twirls through the air before falling into the fog, now billowing below. I just barely have time to grab onto the plank I'm standing on with my right hand as the whole bridge drops from under us. Zach, Noah and I hang on as the bridge swings forward and then slams into the canyon wall.

Janice and Erika scream above us.

"Holy shit!" yells Thomas. I turn my head in panic as I don't know where the dragon is. I can't turn to look back, but when I look to the left, I see the dragon disappear into the distance. It doesn't turn around, though I'm not complaining. It gives me some small hope that it isn't coming back for us just yet. I look up as Thomas and Erika pull Zach to safety. My toes are barely able to catch a sliver of plank, taking an inconsequential amount of my weight. My arm is already straining to hold on, and there isn't much hope of me climbing with my broken hand.

"I can't climb!" I yell out of desperation because honestly, I don't know what I'm going to do. Can the others pull me to safety? Or is this the end? Did I come this far to fall to my death? Was my broken hand the precursor to this moment? Is this my last moment? I want to cry but I know that won't do anyone any good. I can feel my fingers slipping and the muscles in my arm slowly growing more and more tired. I try to grab the plank with my left hand but even that causes a pain to shoot through my whole body that's almost too much to bear. I pull my broken hand back and let it hang uselessly to my side. I don't want to die here. I can practically hear a chorus around me singing "One Day More" from *Les Misérables*.

"Hold on," says Noah, who is climbing steadily

towards me from below. "Just hold on Henry. I'm coming. Just hold on."

"Not much else I can do," I say. But there *is* something else I can do. I can let go. I feel myself wanting it more by the second. I wonder if this is my mind's way of accepting my fate. Am I coming to terms with my own inevitable death? Am I making peace with the fact that I'll never have closure with Zach? That I'll never go to college? Never have my first kiss? My first love?

My little finger slips free of the board, and now I'm only holding on with three fingers. "Hold on!" chant the voices of Thomas, Erika, Janice and even Zach. They're all rooting for me and I'm failing them.

"Do not let go, Henry," says Noah. He's close now. I close my eyes as if keeping them open takes too much away from my efforts to continue holding on. I can hear his voice as if we were right next to each other. A stray thought passes my mind like a butterfly on a spring day. I'd like very much to be next to Noah. Talking about nothing and everything and sharing an iced coffee on a hot day. Laughing at jokes only we understand.

"I'm sorry," I say. I think I say it. I hear myself say it, but I don't even know who I'm apologizing to. My friends? Myself?

My fingers slip.

I open my eyes to look up at everyone for the last time. To witness them as I fall. It's so surreal. It's like I'm floating backwards, like it's the easiest thing in the world. My body slams into Noah who's not far below me at all and the impact pulls him free of the bridge. Damn. Now I have to die with the guilt of knowing I took Noah with me. At least I'll know someone in the afterlife. Even if it is just Noah. Even if he might hate me forever for killing him. He probably could have climbed to safety if not for me. For some reason, thinking about Noah forces the image of Vincent's eyes to appear in my mind. Like maybe somewhere out there he's jealous of not being my dying thought. I wonder if Vincent will be sad when he finds out I didn't make it.

We fall into the fog and then slam hard onto our backs much sooner than I expected. The air is knocked from my lungs on impact. The fact that I have breath at all makes me realize we're still alive after all. In fact, the soft ground helped to cushion our landing. Is it possible that the ground was actually much closer than we all thought? That idea is too good to be true. Not long after, what I initially mistook for oddly absorbent ground begins to move. Not like an earthquake or a tremor. More like the feeling of landing on a very soft ascending elevator. The sudden motion causes me to gasp. Panic-stricken, I push myself up to a sitting position. Our landing spot stops moving, and I look out ahead of me, right into an enormous grey skinned face, complete with a wide nose, a thick beard, two gigantic antlers protruding from thick grey hair, and two very large, amber eyes.

NINE

I stare into the giant's eyes. It's a completely different feeling than staring into the dragon's eye back at the lab. The dragon's gaze was the sort of gaze that hunts down Frodo on his way to Mordor. The giant, on the other hand, looks at us curiously as if we might just be the strangest thing he's ever seen. I say 'He' because it has a great big bushy beard, but I'll be honest, I don't know much about the facial hair of giants. For all I know, this could be a female.

He cocks his head to the side, and I'm reminded of YouTube videos where corgi puppies do the same in unison, first to the left and then to the right, trying to place a strange noise. However, I wouldn't go so far as to call the giant cute. But at the same time, while it's definitely fugly, I wouldn't say it's scary either. I'm awestruck, but that is to be expected when one sees a giant for the first time, let alone one that is literally right in front of your face.

We've landed in the palm of his hand which is the

size of my Dad's pickup and is also a muted blue-grey color. There are thick calluses coating the skin of his fingers and palm which is also covered in deep set lines. Our flashlights and Mr. Zeckel's bag are nowhere to be seen, probably lost in the fall.

"Murrr," groans the giant, opening his lips in an 'O' shape. The force of his breath pushes on us and I lift my hands to cover my face. Beside me, Noah, who was in the process of standing up, topples back onto his rear end. The giant's breath smells like a mixture of strawberries and freshly cut grass.

"Should we be … scared?" asks Noah. "Because I don't really feel scared and that's sort of weird, right?"

"I don't know," I say. "But I think if this thing was going to eat us, or crush us, or whatever us, it would have already done it." I look at Noah and shrug. "Right?"

"Henry! Noah!" Erika's voice cuts through the fog around us from above. She sounds hysterical and why wouldn't she be? As far as she knows, we've just fallen to our deaths.

"We're okay!" I yell up to her, keeping my eyes fixed on the giant, hoping my yelling doesn't set it off.

"Oh, thank God!" yells Erika. The giant looks upwards as the fog around us begins to clear. Within seconds, we can suddenly see up the top of the canyon's walls. Erika, Thomas, Janice and Zach are all leaning over the edge staring at us. Their eyes go wide when they see the giant looking back at them.

"What the hell is that?" yells Zach.

"I think we made a friend," says Noah. He's finally managed to stand and he's not only smiling but waving at the giant.

"I think friend is a bit of a stretch," I say. "This thing could still crush us to death."

The giant slowly lifts its other hand. I wait for it to come down on us and squash us like the bugs we are to this thing. But instead, the giant moves the hand from side to side, waving back at us.

"Woah!" I say, because this is seriously intense. Not like being-chased-by-a-dragon intense, though. This is more communicating-with-a-new-species intense.

"He waved back," says Noah. I swear I can actually see tears forming in his eyes. Like it's all just too overwhelming for him. "He waved back." He says it again, I guess trying to convince himself this is actually happening. "He . . . he waved . . ."

"I know," I say, hopefully reassuring him that this isn't just a dream.

We don't have much time to revel in the moment because the hand we're standing on suddenly starts to move downwards. I stay seated as Noah crouches so that neither of us goes toppling over the edge. Before long, we're low enough that the giant is looking down at us. When his hand stops moving, I look around to find that we've reached the bottom of the canyon. He tips his hand and spills us out onto the gravelly bank of a small river.

We scramble to our feet as the giant stands back up to its full height. He seems much larger from down here. If I had to guess, I'd say he's about as tall as a ten-story building. The canyon walls are even higher. In short, the fact that we're alive right now is a miracle. A thick brown cloth is wrapped around the giant's waist, covering its giant unmentionables. That's about the politest way I can put it. The end of the cloth hangs between its muscular legs and sways in the gentle breeze that is slowly but surely carrying the thick fog out of the canyon.

The giant waves down at us one more time. We wave back enthusiastically. It then turns on its large bare feet and starts down the slight hill, stomping through the river which runs down the center of the canyon as though it were a mere trickling stream. It's not until now with the fog nearly gone that I look down the canyon to see that he's actually following behind a whole line of other giants, all with various hues of skin. One is green, another is a fleshy pink, and the one furthest from us is a subtle lavender. They all have large antlers, bushy beards and bare chests with muscular torsos. I can't help but wondering if these are the men heading off to find their lady friends. Or maybe their men friends. There could be gay giants, right? The ground rumbles softly as they walk away. Despite their huge size, they actually have a light step.

I watch as the giant who saved us reaches the green one and gives his cohort a hearty wave. The other giant gives him a peculiar look at first, then lifts his hand and waves back. Pretty soon they're all waving.

"Look at that," says Noah. "I'm a trendsetter . . . for giants."

"I wonder if you can put that on a college app," I say. We both laugh.

"Guys!" yells Zach from high above. His voice echoes down the canyon. "Are you still alive down there?"

"We're fine!" I yell up.

"Do you see a way up?"

We look around but it's not like there's a ladder or a walkway or anything. "No! We'll have to head down the canyon and see if we can meet up with you guys."

"But it's almost dark," says Noah loudly so that everyone above us can be part of the conversation. "We should all find a place to rest for the night and then we'll try to meet up in the morning!"

"You expect us to sleep out here?" shrieks Janice.

"It's too dangerous to keep going," says Noah. "Not to mention, I think we could all use a little rest." He's not wrong. Even now I can feel my whole body begging to lay down. "Let's take shifts keeping watch. Just in case."

The four above us are quiet for a moment. Then Zach calls back down. "Okay, we're going to stay close to the canyon and find a place to dig in for the night. We'll follow the cliff wall in the morning and keep an eye out for you guys." There's another pause. "Stay safe!"

"You too!" I call. I don't really know what's going on between me and Zach at this point, but I for sure want him to live long enough that we can hash it out.

"Be nice to Henry!" yells Erika. Noah raises an eyebrow as my face flushes. "He's a gentle soul!"

"Who's Henry?" asks Noah with a sly grin on his face.

"I'm fine, Mom!" I yell back to Erika.

I can hear her laugh, but it fades as they leave the cliff behind.

Noah laughs as he takes a few steps up the slope, then leans down and picks up Mr. Zeckel's pack along with both our flashlights, which are strewn across the ground where they landed when we fell. He checks one of the lights to find the bulb broken and tosses it aside. Then he throws me the other one. I don't catch it, obviously. But it doesn't break on impact with the gravelly ground, so I pick it up.

"Nice catch," he mocks.

"I can't really catch things," I say.

"Is that because you're a gentle soul?"

"It's because ... I don't know. I've just never been able to catch things, okay? My brain reacts before my hands and I end up reaching out long before I should and then I miss it."

"Noted." He trudges past me as he throws the backpack over his shoulder. I follow after him and together we descend the slight incline alongside the river as the giants fade into the distance ahead of us.

Night comes faster than I'm expecting. Unlike nighttime back in Orlando, or civilization really, the darkness envelops us from all sides. The only light at all comes from the stars and moon above which, thanks to zero light pollution, are the clearest I've ever seen them. The sky looks like a black canvas spackled with fairy dust. I leave my flashlight off as we follow the river. Something about walking by the light of the stars and the moon feels almost magical. And isn't that the whole point of this place? To experience magic?

We come by a large cave in the wall of the canyon

and both stop. I turn on my flashlight and beam it into the cave. I'm almost surprised to see that there's not a hideous creature waiting inside to devour us. The cave is empty, and my light easily hits the back of the cave which isn't too far from the opening.

"Can't imagine we're going to find a better place to camp," I say.

"Agreed," says Noah approaching the cave entrance. "Let's check it out."

The opening is actually about two feet off the ground. Noah tosses the backpack in first and then lifts himself into the cave. Then he reaches a hand out to help me up. I take it with my unbroken hand, and he pulls me up beside him. We don't let go of each other's hands right away even once I'm safely inside. Our fingers linger over each other and find themselves interlocking. And it's not super awkward either. It's almost like we've just found a brief moment of comfort in each other. "Your hands are super soft," he says. I can feel his thumb caressing my own.

Not knowing if it's a compliment or not, I say, "Thanks. I use lotion." What? Did those words just come out of my mouth? What the hell, mouth? I thought we were on the same team.

He smiles almost shyly at me and then breaks away, pulling his hand from mine and picking up the backpack.

156

He moves further into the cave until he reaches the back where he places his hand on the wall. "Feels dry. We shouldn't get drowned out in the middle of the night by rising tide or whatever."

"Well that's good," I say because honestly, I would never have even thought to check the wall for residual wetness as a sign for possibly drowning in our sleep. "At least that's one crisis averted."

"One of how many?" he asks.

"One is better than none."

"True." He sets the backpack down, then starts to rummage through it. He pulls out the lighter and a large manila envelope filled with papers. "Something tells me Mr. Zeckel won't need our Social Studies homework anymore."

"Guess not," I say with a lump in my throat.

He crumples up several sheets of paper and makes a little stack of them in the center of the cave floor. It looks like a trash pyramid. He then removes several yellow wooden pencils—the old-school kind, not the mechanical ones—and places them on top of the paper so that they all point towards the center. Finally, he flicks the lighter and then touches the flame to the crumpled paper closest to him. The paper ignites, and the fire slowly spreads to the rest of the paper as well as the pencils. He sits back and holds out his hands as if to say, 'look what I did.'

"Hmm!?" he says, impressed with himself.

"Very impressive," I say. "If I had a cookie, I'd give it to you. Well, actually I wouldn't, but that's because I would've already eaten it. Sorry."

"Stone cold. I built you a fire, and you ate my cookie?"

"It's nothing personal. I just like cookies more than fires."

"A cookie won't keep you alive."

"I disagree. What if I was starving to death?" I argue.

"Fair enough." He reaches into his pocket and pulls out his cell phone. He flicks up on the screen and it comes to life. To my surprise, the screen isn't even cracked.

"Wait," I say a little taken aback. "You've had a phone this whole time?"

"Yeah, but no service. Barely any juice. I was trying to wait for the power to come back on, but at this point the battery's gonna die by morning either way. Thing's old. Barely holds a charge even when I'm not being chased around a tropical island."

"So, what do you plan to do with it in here? Do you have some cool trick where you build a fort out of it?"

"You'll see." He swipes a couple of times and then taps the screen. A piano starts to play against what sounds like the static feedback of a record player. I instantly recognize the song. *Preach* by Keiynon Lonsdale. One of his earlier songs. He was the one of the first gay celebrities I really connected with. One of the only ones that wasn't white too. You could say that gave him a pretty special place in my heart.

"Good song," I say.

"I know," he says and there's a slight air of cockiness to his voice.

I roll my eyes and go to sit beside him on the floor. "You really like music, huh? You've always got your earphones in whenever I see you."

"Music helps me process," he says. "Or maybe it's how I cope? I don't really know. I'm not spiritual or anything, but if there is such a thing as a soul, I think mine is happiest when I've got a good song playing in my ears."

It's not until I'm sitting that I realize just how completely exhausted I am. I lean my head back and rest it on the rocky wall, letting my eyes close. It's definitely not as comfortable as a pillow, but it certainly feels great to just sit, breathe and not be chased by terrifying monsters. I open my eyes and look at Noah, who's staring at me *again*. I should be used to it by now, but I'm just not. Especially since I work so hard to avoid eye contact in my day to day life. It just unnerves me. If we're going to be cooped up in this cave together, I have to confront him about it. After all, it's not like confronting Zach. Noah has nowhere to run at this point and we don't really have all the baggage to make things messy.

"Why do you do that?" I ask.

"Do what?"

"Stare at me."

"Sorry," he says, turning away.

"You do it a lot."

"I don't usually realize I'm doing it," he says. "Not sure if that makes it any better."

"It doesn't. It actually kind of freaks me out."

Noah sighs. "I'm sorry, it's just . . ."

"We're sort of stuck here for the night, so you might as well just tell me."

He massages the back of his neck. "You know I mentioned my ex earlier?"

"Yeah?"

"Well I stare at you because . . . you look a lot like him."

This catches me off guard. "Your . . . ex was Asian?"

Noah lets out a short laugh. "No. His family was from Mexico. We met when I was still living in Denver. Lots of Latino guys there, I guess."

"So . . . I look Mexican?" I'm starting to feel some

serious concern that this guy can't tell brown people apart.

"No, not at all. I don't mean you look like him *physically*." He sighs. "It's hard to explain . . ."

"Oh, you mean he was a twink?" the gay term for scrawny guys like me.

"No!" Noah laughs. "Well yeah, he was but . . . just let me finish." He crumples up a few more pieces of paper and throws them into the fire. He watches them burn, crinkling and turning black at the edges. "The way you walk. The way you smile. The way you look away when someone looks at you. The way you slump your shoulders when you sigh. Like it takes your whole body just to exhale. Even the way you roll your eyes when you're annoyed." He smiles, and I feel like his thoughts are a million miles away. "I stare at you because it's like I'm seeing him one more time. And sometimes I need that to keep going. To keep standing up straight."

"I . . ." I want to say something, but I'm not sure what to say. I feel like I've just been dealt a massive blow. Like someone's just punched me in the gut and the air hasn't quite returned to my lungs. It's clear that he still has feelings for his ex. "Is that . . . a good thing?" He talks as if it is, but if I had an ex, I don't think I'd want to have to think about them every time I saw a certain person. "I mean, if you like this guy so much, why aren't you still with him?"

Noah bites his bottom lip. "I didn't really have a choice."

I give him a confused look, hoping he'll explain.

"He, um . . ." Noah looks down at his hands as if the answer might be written on them. He runs his thumb over the tips of his finger, one at a time. Finally, he clears his throat and continues. "He died."

"Oh," I say. Because what else can I say to that? Aside from coming out to my super conservative Mom, I don't really have much drama in my life. But this is like *Spring Awakening* level baggage. I don't really know how to process it in real life. "I'm . . . sorry." And I mean it. I'm sorry that anyone ever has to feel pain or suffering.

"It's okay," he says. "I mean, it's not, but it's . . . it's part of who I am now, I guess. I remember waking up a week after the crash and realizing that for the rest of my life, I'm gonna be someone who lost the first person they ever said, 'I love you' to. For the rest of my life, that moment was going to define me no matter what."

I'm about to do something I do not do with people I barely know. The very thought of doing it makes me tense, but I do it anyway because it just feels like the thing I'm supposed to do in this moment. Something I *want* to do. I scoot closer to him and place my hand on his back, right between his shoulder blades. Touching other people to comfort them may be second nature to a lot of people. But to me, it's something that requires a lot of willpower. I'm entering their bubble, but more importantly, I'm letting them into mine.

"That's why I changed schools in the middle of the semester. I tried to make things work back in Denver but . . . I just couldn't figure it out. I started hanging with a bad group of guys. Started d0ing stupid shit. My parents saw the signs that I was heading in a bad direction, and I guess they'd been looking to move to Florida anyway. My mom friggin' loves Disney." He lets out a stifled laugh and breathes out a long steady breath. He shakes his head, shaking off the heaviness of his words. "Look, Henry, I'm sorry I stare at you. And . . . I'm sorry I just unloaded all of that on you."

Preach finishes up and the next song plays, *Normal* by AJR. I really wanted to go see them in concert but couldn't scrounge up enough cash to make it happen. So far, Noah is two for two on the shuffle test.

"It's okay," I say. "Sometimes you just need to get a load off." My eyes go wide. "Oh my God. That totally sounds like a line out of porno."

"Yes, it does," laughs Noah.

"Forget I said it!" We both laugh. "And as far as the

163

staring thing, I get it. I think I get it, anyway. Honestly, as much as I hate it, I actually kind of like it."

"That makes no sense," he laughs.

"Okay, so it's creepy that you stare at me."

"Wow, harsh."

"Especially knowing that you're thinking of your dead ex."

"Cold *and* harsh."

"*But* there *is* something nice about being noticed."

"So, you like being the center of attention?" he asks skeptically.

"I mean, who doesn't? Sure, not everyone wants to be the class clown, but everyone likes a little attention now and then. So, I don't love being stared at. But I *do* like being seen."

Noah looks right into my eyes and I swear to God, I see a sparkle of light in their emerald depths. An image of Vincent shoves its way into my mind, almost forcefully. I look away guiltily. For some reason, it feels almost wrong to look at another guy. But I don't know why that is.

"You're weird about eye contact, aren't you?" he asks.

"Yeah."

"Why?"

"It's a stupid reason."

"Sure, but you should still tell me."

"Why?" I ask, incredulously.

"Because we're all alone in this cave, and if you don't, the conversation will end and then things will be way more awkward than they already are."

"Touché."

"Come on. Just tell me."

I sigh. "I feel like, if someone looks me in the eyes, they're gonna see past all my bullshit and realize I'm actually just as awful as everyone else."

"You think you're awful? You think *everyone* is awful?"

Oh man, now I have to tell him my theory. I hate that learning about his dark and twisty secrets has opened the door for him to learn about mine. "So, I have this theory that we're all born terrible and that we have to work really hard to be good. Like, humanity is preordained to be garbage."

"Wow," he says with a shocked smile. "That is super depressing." We both laugh as *Summertime* by Childish Gambino starts to play. That's three, Noah Henson.

"I don't know if I think people are inherently good or bad," he starts. "But what I do believe is that people are always more than we give them credit for. I believe the second you categorize someone into a bucket, you deny them the chance to be everything else they might be. Stylish, beautiful, ugly, cool, lame, straight, gay, good . . . or bad. I believe labels are pointless because people aren't just one thing. They aren't even five things. I believe people are millions of things and the millions of things we are change every second of every day for our whole life."

"That is incredibly deep," I say. "It's like you're—" I hold up my hand like I'm writing out a headline. "Powered by belief."

He chuckles. "I usually give that speech to guys over dinner if I want them to kiss me afterwards."

My mouth drops open. "Shut the fuck up. You do not!" I don't love the word 'fuck' but sometimes it's necessary.

"I totally do," he says and we both laugh. Our eyes meet again, and once again, I look away.

But this time, he slides his hand under my chin and gently lifts my face so that my eyes meet his. We stare at each for what feels like a lifetime.

"You're staring again," I say. My voice shakes. I'm not sure why. Am I nervous or scared or excited? Or maybe, like Noah said, I'm all those things and more.

"I'm not, you are," is his answer.

Right then, *Fix You* by Coldplay comes on over the phone speakers. I gasp. "Oh my God. This is literally my favorite song of all time."

"You're lying," he says, looking down at his phone.

"Nope. I love it. I probably listen to it every single day."

"What a sad song to listen to everyday," he says. "No wonder you're so tragic."

"I'm tragic? You have a dead ex and you're still a teenager! Speak for yourself." I let the song wash over me and soak it in. "It's a sad song, sure, but it's also hopeful," I say, defensively. "It's like, happy-sad. Like the end of a great book or the last day of vacation."

"Well my phone is on one percent, so I hope you enjoy it to its fullest." He places the phone back on the ground and throws another paper into the dwindling fire.

Something about this day and this night and the fire and my favorite friggin' song suddenly causes inspiration to come over me. I stand up and hold out my hand, the one that's not turning all shades of blue. Then, I gulp down all my fear, anxiety and worry and say: "Dance with me."

"Dance with you?" asks Noah, looking up at me like I'm a crazy person. "Have the pencil fumes caused you to actually lose your mind?"

"Don't be a dick," I say. "Come on. We're in the middle of a zoo for mythical creatures. We almost died today like ten times. We just escaped a dragon by falling into a giant's hand, and the very last song your phone is playing is my absolute favorite song in the universe.

"I have spent my whole life wasting moments like this because I'm too neurotic or stressed out or anxious. And ... I'm tired of it. I don't want to waste another moment, because we still have half a park full of man-eating beasts to cross, and we might not have a whole lot of moments left. I can't waste *this*. I won't. So just stop acting cool and aloof for like three minutes, and dance with me." I stretch my fingers, inviting him once more. "Please?"

He breathes a long sigh and shakes his head. But then he stands up and approaches me. At first, we aren't really sure where to put our hands. I don't know what his slow dancing experience has been, but mine is dancing with Aunt Ruby at my cousin's wedding. Eventually my hands end up around his neck and his end up around my waist. As the guitar solo begins, we pull each other close and sway next to the paper fire. I press my face into his neck and all the stress and terror of the day finally hits me. As the words "tears stream down your face," play, tears actually stream down my face. He's crying too. I know it because I feel the wetness on my cheek, and I hear him sniffling as we continue to sway.

The song ends and on the last note, the phone screen goes black, except for the outlined image of a battery, empty. Even in the silence, we don't stop swaying in each other's arms. We continue like this as tiny specks of burning paper float up around us. Sounds of cicadas and crickets echo in from outside, playing a concert of their very own.

Eventually, the fire burns itself out. Only then do we settle back onto the floor, leaning our backs against the wall of the cave. We don't talk about what just happened between us. We don't even acknowledge it. Like it's this fragile thing that could break if we confront it.

"I'll take first watch," he says.

"You sure?"

"Yeah, you get some rest." It's dark now. So dark that I can't see his face. But I feel like he's smiling. At least, I hope that he's smiling. Maybe I think he is because I am. I lean my head back, but it droops, little by little, sliding against the wall until finally it finds a resting place on his soft shoulder. Only then does sleep take me.

TEN

My eyes blink open as the morning sun cuts in through the end of the cave. The first thing I hear is gentle snoring, and I look over to see that Noah has fallen asleep next to me. I guess the fact that we survived the night means it's okay that he completely failed to wake me up to stand watch. I'm prepared to forgive him for falling asleep until I feel a strange wetness on my arm. It reminds me of my great aunt Sylvie's dog, Paquin, who was always a very enthusiastic licker. I turn over, putting me face to face with a creature that would be terrifying except that it looks just as startled by me as I am by it.

I recognize the creature immediately by its jet-black hairless skin, pointed cat-like face and large ears that resemble a bat's wings. The chupacabra's most pronounced features are the intermittent quills which poke sparsely along its back like a balding porcupine. The chupacabra lets out a sound that is halfway between a cat's meow and a bird's chirp and then skitters backwards. Two more like it pounce away from Noah's other side, and together the posse bounds out of the cave and disappears.

Noah smacks his lips sleepily as he wakes up. He yawns and looks at me. His half-asleep emerald eyes peering out from behind his drooping eyelids are probably the most seductive things I've ever seen. And the most annoying part is that he's not even trying to be seductive. He's just trying to be awake.

"What'd I miss?" he asks with a long droll in his voice.

"You missed waking me up to take the next watch, for starters," I snap. I'm not really mad but I put a little sass into my voice for good measure. I feel it's my duty to perfect the art of sass before I go to college.

"Oh crap," he says, becoming more alert. "I must have fallen asleep."

"Yeah, sure. Well, I woke up just in time to stop you from being eaten by chupacabras." The look on his face is priceless. He's scared and embarrassed all at once. Like a child who has just broken a Christmas ornament by playing swords in the house, which they knew was strictly against the rules. And yes, I am speaking from experience.

"Seriously?" He looks around, expecting them to still be here.

"Relax. They look a lot scarier than they are. And they actually only eat hair. Not blood like all the folktales

171

would have you believe. The worst they would have done was shave your arms for you."

He runs a hand along his arm, lightly touching the thin hair there. "That's disgusting."

"Fish gotta swim. Chupacabras gotta eat hair. That's life." I stand up and stretch my arms. Sleeping in a cave has done me no favors. Everything hurts.

"Life is disgusting," says Noah. He shudders as he stands up. Then he grabs the backpack by one of its straps and throws it over his shoulder.

I pull the bandage wrapped around my broken hand free and immediately wish I hadn't. My hand is swollen to double its size and is a dark midnight blue. It looks like something out of a horror movie and my stomach can't help but churn at the sight.

"How is it?" asks Noah.

"Bad," I say, turning away from him and rewrapping it with the now dirty bandage. Even the touch of the cloth stings.

"We need to get back to the Palace," says Noah. "Today."

"I'm game if you are," I say. Together, we go to the edge of the cave. Noah jumps down to the gravelly riverside path first, then helps me down. I stumble in my landing and fall into him. But unlike last night, when our

172

hands lingered, I pull back. Everything feels heavier in the daylight. Like last night was part of some zero-consequence dream. We were exhausted, but now that we're rested everything seems too real.

I keep thinking about Vincent, and how he'd feel if he found out that Noah and I had danced and shared secrets and slept next to each other. I almost feel like I can sense Vincent looming over my shoulder, scrutinizing every move I make. Daylight brings out complications that the night was kind enough to hide in the shadows.

"Hopefully the canyon ends down here and we can meet up with the others," says Noah.

"Right."

"You okay?"

Am I? I don't really know. Physically I guess you could say I'm a little busted. But emotionally? I'm not a wreck, but I'm also not great either. Is that the definition of okay? "Yeah," I say, because it's easier than explaining the vicious cycle of self-doubt that's rising in me like a *wingardium leviosa* spell has been cast on it.

"Okay," he says. We head off down the path. The air is warm and feels good on my face. A family of bunyips appears and paddles alongside us in the river. I recognize them from pictures; they're really odd looking. They're about the size of a seal, except that they have four legs and a tail. Their faces are long and rat-like with two beady eyes and two tusks like a walrus. Red hair runs down their back in a mane, and their skin is a muddy brown color. The weird thing is that they sort of always look like their smiling contently. They're not too aggressive, but supposedly they can be pretty territorial. We keep our distance and they keep theirs.

The river and the path wind steadily along and then veer left. As we round the bend, we can see that the ravine eventually opens up to a wide valley with tall green grass which bends gently in the breeze. Butterflies and bees fly over the sea of green, stopping occasionally to collect nectar from the many small white flowers which stretch their petals out to greet the sun. I honestly wouldn't be surprised to see a double rainbow arcing over the field. It's as if we've stumbled on paradise.

Despite a night of sleep, I'm still exhausted. Even so, I quicken my pace, drawn forward by the lush landscape.

We don't really talk. There might be some tension between us, but it's hard to tell because the babble of the river, the ambient chirping of birds, and the crunching of our feet on the gravelly path devour the silence between us.

We reach the end of the ravine where the cliff walls have become much shorter. The path leads us into the valley as the river curls into a small waterfall and then deposits itself into a large lake. The water reflects the sky off its perfectly smooth surface.

"Wow," says Noah. "This is amazing. Like, I could live here."

"And I bet you could get a good deal considering all the man-eating monsters running around," I say with a grin. It's a joke, but I can't help but feel a little nervous. After all, the last place we should probably spend a lot of time is in the middle of a wide-open field where anything can find us with no place to hide.

Noah suddenly lets out a short gasp. I turn to find him staring out into the field with his mouth hanging open. I follow his gaze, stopping when I see what's dropped his jaw. Standing on a small hill, nibbling brazenly on the long grass, is a shimmering white horse with a long silky main that seems to sparkle in the sunlight. It could easily just be a really pretty horse, except for the long, spiraling horn which protrudes straight up from the center of its head.

"A unicorn," I say in a whisper. Maybe I need to speak its name to fully believe that one is standing here in front of me. As you might expect, unicorns are the single most beloved creature in Mythos. They're the *Frozen* of the Mythos park. Unicorn merchandise always outsells every other item in the shops by a landslide. People spend their entire life savings purely to come see one and then cry when they see them for the first time. And now, I finally understand why. It's the most beautiful creature I've ever laid eyes on.

Noah starts to walk forward slowly, like maybe he's being drawn to it by some unforeseen force.

"Noah?" I seriously think he might have been hypnotized.

"Yeah?" he says, still moving forward.

"What are you doing?"

"I think . . . I think we could ride it back," he says.

"Are you insane? Have you actually lost your mind?"

"They're supposed to be friendly right?" he finally spares a glance back at me.

"Sure, in *stories*," I say. "But they're a lot of things in stories. All these animals are. When I was little, my grandma used to read me this book where a unicorn could fly, heal the sick and shoot magic out of its horn, but that doesn't mean they actually can." I don't tell Noah that the book, *My Friend the Unicorn*, was always dear to my heart. Maybe it's because it was the only kid's book at my grandma's place for a while, so she read it to me like a broken record. But to this day, I still have that book memorized. And looking at this unicorn now, I honestly believe they *could* heal a person. This creature looks like it might have been crafted from sheer goodness and light.

"Just . . . trust me on this one," says Noah.

"Trust you?" I feel frustrated. "Trust you to what? Get yourself impaled by a unicorn?"

"It's not going to impale me," he says.

"How do you know that?"

"I just know!" The look in his eyes is pure desperation. He doesn't give me another opportunity to object. He turns on his heels and stomps off across the field, heading straight for the unicorn.

I stay put for as long as I can convince myself to not go with him. "Dammit." I launch into a jog to catch up.

We walk over one small hill and then up the second, at the top of which is the shimmering white horse. As he gets near, Noah's pace finally slows. The unicorn is still grazing, but as soon as we're within a few feet of it, it finally lifts its head and looks at Noah. They both freeze, as if they're having the world's first unicorn versus human staring contest. I stand just behind Noah and I can feel my chest tighten as I hold my breath, waiting for something horrible to happen.

Noah moves forward like a sloth I once saw in a nature documentary, slow and steady. First one foot, then the other, then the first once more. It seems like several long minutes pass until at last, Noah stands directly in front of the unicorn. The horse's nose hovers right in front of Noah's face. It's easy to look only at the unicorn because, well, it's just so insanely majestic that it's hard to look away.

But I force myself to look at Noah. I take in this person that I only met two days ago. The kind of person who could be attacked by mythical creatures all day and then, on the very next day, have the courage to walk right up to one. In his own way, Noah is also a majestic, beautiful creature. He's just as captivating to me as the unicorn that stands before us.

I feel Vincent again. As if he's watching me admiring this other guy. As if he's jealous. Vincent's face flashes before my eyes and then vanishes. Great, now my guilt is making me hallucinate. I shake off the feeling of being watched and refocus on Noah.

His hands are shaking as he lifts them both up, palms out. I can hear each of his breaths—deep intakes of air followed by slow, calculated exhalations through his mouth. I keep thinking the unicorn is either going to head butt him, which would kill him instantly, or turn tail and run. But it just stands there, as if waiting expectantly.

Noah brings both hands to either side of the unicorn's long face and holds them mere inches away from the beast. He closes his eyes, leaving the next moments to fate. As he exhales, he brings his hands in until they land softly on the unicorn's cheeks. The unicorn's head bows slightly, placing it level with Noah's, and then the greatest surprise of all happens. Noah leans forward and places his forehead against the unicorn's. Watching him, I feel like I can see the moment that every muscle, every fiber, of his body relaxes.

I move around Noah so that I'm standing next to the right side of the unicorn's head. Its mane, which hangs down over its thick neck, looks as though it has been sprinkled with glitter which sparkles in the light. Tears are running unashamedly down Noah's face.

"Thank you," he mutters under his breath. "Thank you, thank you, thank you." His words run together and become gentle sobs.

I feel like I'm watching a deeply personal moment. This is what it might have felt like if someone were to walk in on the night I came out to my parents. It almost feels wrong for me to be standing here. I'm not sure what makes me reach out and touch the unicorn. It's almost like second nature, like the way you might lean on a banister just because it was there.

The moment my right hand touches the creature's neck, a flood of warmth surges through my body. I feel myself gasp for air, not because I can't breathe, but because the feeling is so incredibly intense and overwhelming that it takes me by surprise. It feels like every good thing that could ever happen to me is happening right in this moment. My Mom has accepted me being gay and I've gotten into NYU and I've fallen in love and I have two amazing kids who grew up to make the world a better place. I feel all of it in that moment, and I know why Noah is crying. I don't know how I know, but I know. He's seeing the love he lost one last time. He's getting the ending that was robbed from him. He's getting to say goodbye.

RAAAAWWWWR!! I pull my hand away and turn to see a dragon, the same one from yesterday by the looks of it, bursting through the tree line on the far side of the valley. The moment I pull away, the warmth diminishes, but doesn't abandon me completely. My heart feels like it could burst from joy; like I'm a battery charged with love.

The dragon roars again and this time I see a whole herd of unicorns galloping towards us and away from the distant dragon, trying desperately to escape it. Our own unicorn neighs and then gallops away, leaving us behind. Noah looks up at me and smiles as he wipes his eyes.

"That was . . ." he says.

"Amazing," I say.

He nods, collecting himself. "We need to run now."

"Agreed." No sooner is this decision made do several unicorns come barreling over the ridge at us. We turn to run back down the hill as fast as we can, looking back now and then in order to avoid being trampled by the white steads which race by us at incredible speed.

There's another roar, and then I hear the sound of a loud crash like a semi-truck has just dropped to the ground from high above. I stop and turn back.

"Henry!" yells Noah. "What are you doing? We have to go! We're too exposed out here."

But I barely hear him, because I'm focused on the dragon. I've stopped to stare at it. The monster that's been trying to kill us for the past twenty-four hours. Except right now it's not trying to kill us at all. I'm not entirely sure what it's doing exactly. I imagine a dog rubbing its neck and scruff along the ground, trying to scratch an itch it can't quite reach, except on a much larger scale. The dragon stands up straight once more, stretches its neck upwards, and lets out another mighty roar. Sunlight glints off of something in the base of the dragon's neck. The dragon again plunges its neck into the ground and continues to shuffle around, trying to scratch itself, or perhaps—I realize—dislodge the shiny object.

I walk towards the dragon. I don't know how much

control I even have over my own two legs at this point. It's as if my auto-pilot switch has been turned on.

"Henry!" yells Noah again, but my ears have turned off the sound of his voice, or at least dialed him down. I can't quite explain this feeling that's come over me. It's as if touching the unicorn has given me some deep desire to do good. And seeing the dragon now, clearly upset by whatever is irritating its neck, makes me not just want to help it, but *need* to. The dragon beats its wings and the air whooshes by me. The bandage on my broken hand, loosened by the wind, pulls away and flutters off in the wind. I quickly glance at my hand to find that it's no longer swollen or even discolored. In fact, it's been completely healed.

I look up, still several paces from the dragon, and continue forward. As I reach it, the dragon looks down at me apprehensively and then snaps its jaws at me. I dodge out of the way, rolling to the side so that it just misses me. The dragon seems barely interested in my presence to begin with, as if snapping at me is more for the purpose of getting me to leave it alone, rather than to actually harm me. I'm fairly certain that if it really wanted to kill me right now, I'd be dead. Somewhere behind me, Noah is yelling at the top of his lungs. To me, his voice is like the ambient hum of an air conditioner or overhead fan, heard but barely registered.

I get back on my feet and move past the dragon's front leg to reach the spot which glimmered in the sun. The thick shard of glass impaled in the beast's scaly green neck isn't hard to spot. Dark red blood has dried around it where it splattered after the wound was initially inflicted. I remember the dragon bursting through the wall of the lab and shattering the window. I'm guessing that was when this happened, but it could have also been the result of the dragon escaping captivity after the power went down.

The dragon rolls so that it can drag its neck along the ground again. I move out of the way and follow the dragon as it shuffles forward. When it rolls back up, there is a deep groove torn through the grass. I notice that the glass shard hasn't sunk any deeper into the dragon's neck. Its thick hide is preventing the shard from getting any deeper, but not stopping the irritation that having it stuck there is causing.

I move swiftly up to the dragon, using its leg and scales to climb up to its neck. Then I place both hands on the glass shard and pull. Some part of me knows that what I'm doing is absolutely insane and that I am most likely about to get eaten, but the warmth of the unicorn still lingers in my veins, driving me fearlessly forward.

I pull with everything I've got. I grit my teeth and feel

my arms strain as my fingers slip across the glass' smooth surface. Just as I'm about to lose my grip entirely, the shard pulls lose and rips free of the dragon's hide.

I topple with the large piece of glass in my arms back to the ground. The dragon twists its neck around staring right at me. With its tooth-filled mouth so close I could reach out and touch it; the dragon roars at me. I cover my ears and squeeze my eyes shut, which doesn't help to dampen the torrential wave of sound in the slightest. The roar ends and before I can open my eyes, I feel a warm, sticky wetness on my cheek. I open my eyes to find that the dragon's snake-like tongue has slid out of its mouth and is licking my face. No amount of unicorn good vibes can convince me that this isn't incredibly gross.

"Ew!" The dragon pulls back and blinks once. I just stare up at it. We can't talk or communicate but for some reason, I feel as though we've come to an understanding. The moment is gone before I have time to really process it. The beast turns, flaps its gigantic wings several times, and takes off into the sky.

I pull myself off the ground as Noah runs up to me. "Are you crazy!?" he's both relieved and mortified.

"What? You did it first!" I watch as the dragon flies away.

"To a unicorn! Not a friggin' dragon."

"He needed my help." And that's all it takes to get Noah to stop yelling at me. He inhales like he's about to start again, but then let's the breath out slowly before he gives a single knowing nod. He comes to stand next to me and we both look up as the dragon joins three others of its kind. We watch them soar across the sky. I can't help but feel astonished by these creatures. In the distance, cresting over the treetops, I can just make out the curved shape of the dragon dome.

"They're heading back to the dome," says Noah.

"Yeah."

"Why would they go back to their cage?"

"It's the only home they've ever known," I say. "Sure, to us, it's a way to confine them, but to them, everything outside it is totally foreign." I imagine the sudden freedom must be exciting and terrifying all at once.

I feel Noah's fingers slip into mine and then close so that he's holding my hand tightly in his. "Your theory's bullshit," he says.

I turn my head to look at him. "Excuse me?"

"Your theory about people being born inherently bad."

"Oh yeah?"

"There is no way you were born inherently bad, Henry Lau. No one tries so hard to be good that they'd

185

pull a shard of glass out of a dragon's neck, knowing full well the dragon could eat them. That kind of goodness is built in from birth."

I smile as we watch the dragons on the horizon. We can still just make them out, zipping in and out of the clouds.

An unfamiliar sound enters our ears. It doesn't sound like any animal we've heard so far. It's not a growl or a grunt or a hiss. This sounds more like an engine revving and it sounds like it's getting closer. We both turn, our hands separating, as an enclosed jeep bursts through the tree line, turns and skids to the side, coming to a halt right in front of us. The jeep's doors fly open as Erika, Zach, Janice and Thomas explode out of the vehicle, running towards us.

"Henry!" Erika screams as she jumps into my arms, wrapping herself around me like a love python. That's right, I said it. A love python. Zach slaps Noah on the shoulder and Janice smiles and waves at us. Thomas is looking up at the sky, probably thinking of something witty to say about clouds or why the sky is blue. I feel the wet hint of tears welling up in the corner of my eyes. I'm thrilled to see all of them still safe and sound, even Thomas.

"Where did you guys find a jeep?" I ask. "Who

drove?"

"I have a learner's permit," says Thomas.

"So, you drove?" I ask.

"Oh, no," he says and then looks back up at the sky. I take it back. I'm not as thrilled about him being here as I thought.

"I did," says a familiar voice. The driver's side door opens. I gasp in disbelief as a middle-aged man I thought I'd never see again emerges, smiles cheerily, and waves at us.

"Holy shit." Mr. Zeckel, against all odds, is alive.

ELEVEN

"Mr. Zeckel?" I say. "How?"

"Your teacher is pretty spry," he says, and of course he uses the word 'spry.' "I do calisthenics three times a week, weight-training two times a week and yoga on Sundays." This fool puts his palms together in prayer and bows. "Namaste."

"I'm pretty sure Yoga doesn't teach anything about jumping out of a speeding train onto a giant mythical bird and somehow surviving," I say.

"Yoga teaches all things," says Mr. Zeckel, knowing full well he's being obnoxious.

"No offense Mr. Zeckel," sighs Erika. "But for once your students *actually* want to hear what you have to say. Maybe don't squander this moment."

Mr. Zeckel gives her a vicious side-eye and then clears his throat. "Fine, fine," he concedes. "Not much to tell really. I jumped out of the train, grabbed that very large eagle—"

"Roc," I interject.

"Correct, Mr. Lau. Five points to Gryffindor." He gives me a thumbs up and I roll my eyes. "I was apparently too heavy for it, because it wasn't long before we ended up on solid ground. The bird, err, roc, was quite unhappy with the whole thing. Unfortunately, I had to resort to violence, which you kids should never do." He waggles his finger at us, accusingly.

"You punched one of the death eagles," says Zach.

"I defended myself," corrects Mr. Zeckel.

"With your fists," adds Zach.

"Fine," sighs Mr. Zeckel. "Yes, I punched the bird. It was the only way to get it to leave me alone."

"That's badass," says Noah.

"Language Mr. Henson." But Mr. Zeckel has a sly smile on his face because what middle-aged teacher wouldn't appreciate a student calling him badass?

"Anyway, after that I worked my way down the cliffs until I got to the ground level. I was heading towards the dome perimeter when I found a hatch that took me underground. It was late at that point and coming down the cliffs had worn me out, so I decided to rest for the night. At first light, I headed deeper into the underground tunnels. It was pretty dark since all the power was out, but I was able to find my way to a box of flares early on. I took those and followed the signs on the walls until I found a small garage and this jeep." He points to the vehicle behind him with his thumb. "Decided that anyone who had survived could probably make it about halfway across the island in a day, so I cut straight through the middle, hoping I'd run into, well, anyone." He shrugs. "I found these four." He motions towards Zach, Erika, Janice and Thomas. "And they insisted we come and find you and here we are."

"Pretty cool," says Noah. "Though the story definitely peaked at punching a death eagle. I could do without the rest."

"I'm not trying to impress you," snaps Mr. Zeckel. "I'm just telling you how I got here."

"Next time, I'll wait for it to hit streaming," says Zach.

I turn to Zach and Erika and for the first time notice several red patches on their arms and a couple on their faces. The same markings also appear on Thomas and Janice, though Janice definitely has the most of them. She looks like she's broken out in hives. And she seems super miserable about it.

"What the hell happened to you guys?" I reach for Erika's arm and lightly touch one of the marks, not wanting to hurt her. She pulls back instantly, sucking in a breath in pain. "Sorry," I say quickly.

"We ran into some fairies," says Zach. "Mean as hell. I thought fairies were supposed to be all magic and sparkle, but they were more like hatred and pain."

Janice rubs her shoulders, looking away in annoyance and shame. I can't help but notice that she's no longer hanging off of Zach. Maybe something happened between them? In any case, Zach is still wearing the gaudy dragon tooth necklace, so they can't be completely done for. After all, if they had called it quits in the woods, he would have thrown that stupid thing away. Or, at least I know I would.

"They were awful, Henry," says Erika. "Like little blue naked devil babies. They were all skin and bones with these creepy bug wings. They came down on us from the trees and started snapping at us with their teeth. You were right. They really were like wasps except much bigger. And there were so many. I'm surprised we got out of there."

"We almost didn't" says Janice. Her tone is icy and cold. "At least some of us almost didn't."

"What is she talking about?" I ask.

"Janice took the worst of it," says Thomas, looking anywhere but at her.

"That's right, I did," she snaps. Her voice sounds like it could be laced with thorns. She's pissed. "The fairies couldn't get enough of me, and where was the person who should have been protecting me?" She looks at Zach and I swear that if looks could kill, he'd drop dead right on the spot.

"Janice, come on," he says. "You know it wasn't like that. Everything was crazy. We were all over the place. I didn't mean to . . ."

"He was off protecting some other girl!" she says, ignoring the fact that he was talking at all.

I look at Erika whose face has turned a bright red. To Janice's point, Erika looks to be the least affected by the fairy attack.

"Janice. I wasn't trying to protect her over you," says Zach desperately.

"Weren't you?" she snaps.

"I'm guessing Thomas over here wasn't helping either?" adds Noah. He has to know he's only making things worse.

"I couldn't really swat away the fairies all that well," says Thomas. Then he turns to Mr. Zeckel. "I suffer from weak joints in both my arms."

"Sounds awful," says Mr. Zeckel sympathetically.

"Right, I forgot," says Noah. "Go on." He motions to Janice.

She stomps over to Zach. "You protected her instead of me! You are the worst boyfriend I have ever had, and I have had a *lot* of boyfriends."

"Yikes," says Noah, in a completely deadpan voice. I want to laugh, but now is definitely not the time or the place. I give him a light slap, because even though I think his reactions are actually really funny, he's only adding fuel to the fire.

"Janice, come on," says Erika. "Give him a break. Things were crazy. We were all just trying to survive. No one was picking sides, okay?"

Janice looks at Erika with tears in her eyes. "Give him a break?" She asks, pointing at Zach. "Give HIM a break? He left me for dead with those monsters and you want me to give him a break? Erika, do you even know what it feels like to have your heart shattered into a million pieces? Do you know what it's like to care for someone and see them run to save someone else?!"

"Yeah Janice! I do! Thanks to you, I fucking do!" yells Erika. She freezes as if she can't believe what she's just said. Zach's face is a mixture of confusion and dread.

"I didn't . . ." starts Erika. She looks at Zach. "I didn't mean . . ."

There's a long silence before Mr. Zeckel breaks it with a sigh. "Yeah, I definitely don't miss being a teenager."

"Can you even remember being a teenager?" asks Noah. "That was like, a super long time ago, right?"

193

"Stop it," I say, playfully slapping Noah. Erika looks at me like I'm some strange foreign object. Then she points at me, then at Noah, then back at me, then proceeds to waggle her finger between the two of us.

"What's this?" she asks. "What's happening here?"

"Nothing's happening," I say. "Put your shame finger back in its holster."

"I mean, I don't know if it's *nothing*," says Noah. I look at him, expecting the sarcastic look he makes when he's joking. But it's a look of hurt.

"I knew it," said Erika.

"What did you know?" I put on the most judgmental face I can muster. "You know nothing. It's nothing."

"I mean . . ." starts Noah.

"Can we talk about this later?" I say, cutting him off. There's obviously something between me and Noah, but I'm not sure if I'm ready for there to actually be *something* between me and Noah. He's still clearly getting over his ex and then there's also Vincent. It's all so overwhelming. Add in the salt and pepper of being in a life or death situation and I can't help but feel as though I've landed at the salad bar of confusion.

Noah's shoulders slump as though I've deflated him. "Yeah . . . okay."

"I think we should table all of this," says Mr. Zeckel.

194

"It's time we headed back to the Palace and rendezvoused with whatever rescue team they've got in place."

"A fine idea, sir," says Thomas heading for the jeep. *This guy.*

We all pile into the jeep without another word to each other. Thomas and Zach sit on the long front seat next to Mr. Zeckel. I sit in the back in the middle seat, with Erika on my lap. Next to me on my left is Janice and on my right is Noah. No one wants to be this close to each other, save for me and Erika. I'm super happy to see that she's alive and I can tell she's happy to see me too. Everyone buckles up and we cross some of the seatbelts to overlap Erika.

"Now normally I wouldn't condone this sort of seating arrangement," says Mr. Zeckel. "But this is an emergency situation we find ourselves in. If I ever catch one of you leaving school as a passenger, or with passengers, sitting on each other's laps, I will pull you over and you will have detention for a month. Are we clear?" He looks back at all of us as we all nod. "Good." He turns the key, and the jeep revs to life. A moment later we're headed down the hill towards the Palace.

TWELVE

The jeep rumbles along down the sloping hills of the valley until we reach the tree line and, much to our surprise, a paved road which takes us into the forest.

"Makes sense that they would have roads on the island," says Thomas. "I mean, the techs and animal handlers have to be able to get around, and I can't imagine they just walk everywhere."

"Is it weird that we haven't seen anyone?" I say. "Like, no helicopters or emergency vehicles? Their response time can't be this slow, can it?" To me, this is super weird because Mythos portrays themselves as so structured, so exacting. Then again, that's how *West World* and *Jurassic Park* were portrayed too. Every valley, mountain and dome is strategically placed. Not to mention the way Dawson Saks often brags about how safe the park is every time he's on TV. The fact that we've been out in the wild for almost two full days now without any sign of rescue means that this place either really wasn't expecting this to happen, or something much worse than a power outage has occurred. I try not to think about what horrible thing that might be. I hope Vincent is okay, wherever he is. Hell, anyone back at the Town Square may very well have been evacuated off the island by now. The next time I see him might be at school.

"Maybe they really thought this was the safest place on Earth," says Mr. Zeckel. "Humanity's biggest threat is very often our hubris. Look at the Titanic."

"Great movie," Janice chimes in. Her cheeks flush and she stares off with a dreamy look in her eyes. "Young Leo."

"The shipwrights were so confident in the ship's inability to sink that they didn't bother equipping it with enough lifeboats. And we all know how that ended."

"But there's no way this is as bad as that," says Erika, still seated in my lap. "I mean, are we really saying this situation could be Leonardo-and-Kate-starring-in-a-movie-about-us bad?"

"Hard to say until we get back to the Town Square," says Mr. Zeckel. "I'm sure there will be someone there who can fill us in on everything that's happened since the train left the station yesterday."

"I want to be played by Zendaya," says Janice, staring out the window at the passing trees.

"Oscar Isaac would make a fine Thomas Ruiz," says

Thomas.

"Well that's optimistic," says Janice.

"Obviously Beyoncé is going to play me," says Erika proudly. "What about you, Henry?"

"Hmm, tough call," I say. Up until a few years ago, there weren't that many Chinese actors that I could reference in a situation like this. But now, thanks to films like *Crazy Rich Asians* and TV shows like *Fresh Off the Boat*, I finally feel like the mainstream media has acknowledged my existence. "I'm gonna have to go with Ludi Lin . . . or Awkwafina." Erika and Zach both laugh.

"Awkwafina's a girl, dude" says Zach, which takes me back a little since he hasn't spoken to me without yelling for a while.

"I know," I say. "But she could totally pull it off." This gets a few more laughs. "How about you?" I ask, poking Noah.

"Oh," he says, surprised by the question. It's almost like he's gotten used to not being part of a group. "I guess, Cole Sprouse?"

"Ohhhh!" we all say, because everyone knows Cole from *Riverdale,* and everyone knows he's crazy hot.

"Who's that?" asks Mr. Zeckel.

"He's on *Riverdale*," says Janice.

"Riverdale? You mean like in *Archie Comics*? Could it

be that I know about something you kids are into?" We all sigh audibly.

"You're hopeless Mr. Zeckel," says Erika shaking her head. "We're talking about a TV show, not some comic book."

He flushes. "You just wait until you're my age," he says. "Your kids will be talking about the newest star or piece of technology and you'll think they're speaking a foreign language. Just you wait." I can't imagine that ever happening, but I suppose it does. Time happens to all of us, whether we like it or not. "How's your hand holding up?" Mr. Zeckel asks, his eyes flicking to me in the rearview mirror.

"Oh," I say, lifting my now completely healed hand. "It's actually fine."

"What!?" exclaims every voice in the jeep. Everyone is in disbelief, especially Noah who reaches over to grab my hand, examining it like a science project.

"It looked like you'd broken it before," says Mr. Zeckel. "I can't believe it healed so quickly."

"When did this happen?" asks Noah, who's completely baffled because only an hour or so ago, we were in the cave and I told him it wasn't looking so good.

"I guess when I touched the unicorn," I say.

"Just to be clear," says Thomas because he must

realize he hasn't spoken in over sixty seconds. "Did you actually *touch* a unicorn or is that a gay euphemism for something?"

"Thomas!" shouts Erika, slapping him in the back of the head.

"Sorry!" he yelps. "I meant LGBTQTA etcetera reference."

"This fucking guy," says Noah under his breath.

"Right?" I say because I'm always thinking that, and Noah just said it!

"Language!" yells Mr. Zeckel.

"Just to be clear," I say, quieting the small uproar overtaking the jeep. "We actually *touched* a unicorn."

"O.M.G. I am so jealous," says Erika, sounding girlier than I'm used to.

"Was it . . . how was it?" asks Janice. I can tell she's shy about asking, maybe because it's so rare for her to actually be interested in something someone else is saying.

"It was . . . sort of unreal," I say.

"Yeah," says Noah. "I really want to be able to describe it, but I don't know if that's even possible."

Janice bites her bottom lip. "I want to pet one," she says and then goes back to staring out the window.

We continue to drive, chatting randomly about what we've seen in the park so far, catching Mr. Zeckel up on the dragon, the kappa and the fate of the train conductor. I think we're all wondering who in our class has survived, but no one is brave enough or ready to start that conversation, so we stick to relatively lighter topics.

The paved road curves through the forest, at one point coming up alongside the third dome, which houses the bird/mammal hybrids. We all lean over to look out the window when several gryphons fly in formation within the dome. They're amazing creatures with the upper body of an eagle and the lower body of a lion. I can't help but be in awe of these mythical beasts, even now after so many others have tried to eat us over the past two days.

"Looks like they decided to stay in their enclosure," says Zach.

"Supposedly they're really laid back as a species," I add. "They probably didn't even try to escape when the power went down."

"Well that's great," says Zach. "I was hoping the one animal we didn't encounter was the one that didn't want to eat us."

"Maybe next time," I laugh.

"Yeah, I'm gonna pass on next time," says Zach. He looks back at me, past Erika who's sitting in my lap and smiles for just a moment. Maybe we're slowly getting back to normal, as if any of this was ever normal. Maybe we're discovering a new normal. Our friendship, not Mythos shutting down or monsters trying to kill us. Just to be clear. Either way, I prefer whatever this is to awkward silences or fighting all the time. His eyes shift to Erika and his face flushes a little before he looks away. I bite my bottom lip; I totally know that look because it's the look I gave Vincent. It's the look I sometimes catch Noah giving me. It's the look of someone longing for someone else. I suddenly realize what should have been obvious all along. Zach's totally into Erika. Considering that they're my two best friends, you'd think I'd have a problem with it, but somehow it all seems okay. I just hope he tells her before Janice gets too attached.

I look over at Janice who's watching the gryphons and their habitat fade behind us. Once they're out of sight, she goes back to watching the trees rush by. The world outside the jeep grows dark as the treetops above us become thick, barely allowing any light through.

"Oh shoot," says Mr. Zeckel as the jeep slows and then comes to a stop. He puts the vehicle into park and removes the key.

"What's happening?" asks Thomas.

"We're low on gas," says Mr. Zeckel.

"Already?" asks Zach, mentally adding up the miles we've driven versus how many miles to a gallon this jeep should be able to get.

"It was low when I found it. Didn't realize we were so far away from the Palace at the time. Not to worry. I loaded a couple of jugs into the trunk just in case. I'll just fill us up and we'll be on our way." He opens the door and slides out of the car, closing the door behind himself. We sit in the silence with only the sound of our breathing and the small creaks the car makes whenever one of us moves to keep us company. But there's also another sound. It's faint, but I swear I hear a noise outside the jeep. It's distant, almost like it isn't there at all. It could easily be in my imagination, but my gut tells me it's not. And while I can't seem to find the words to describe it, I swear it sounds like high-pitched laughter.

Janice looks away from the window, towards the front of the jeep, then she looks at me and Erika. "Do you hear that?" she asks.

The sound starts again and this time we all hear it. It's as if the trees are laughing at us. But it's not just any laugher. It's the highest part of a laugh when someone's laughing so hard they can't breathe. It comes in waves, moving around us. And where at first, I thought it was just one laugh, now it sounds as if several laughs are surrounding us. I turn towards the window next to Janice and lean over her to look outside.

"Um personal space?" she says, but I ignore her. My steady breath fogs the glass.

"Oh no," I say in a whisper, suddenly terrified at the thought of being heard. "Mr. Zeckel." My voice shakes as I slowly turn in my seat to face the back of the jeep.

"What is it?" asks Thomas in a voice that is way too loud.

I turn to him and place a single finger over my lips. He doesn't speak again, and I see him swallow whatever words were about to come out of his mouth. As I turn back, I make sure everyone sees my finger over my lips and understands that now is not the time to make any sound. Mr. Zeckel lifts a red gas can out of the back and we make eye contact. I mouth the words 'we're being hunted' to him. He nods, not understanding what I said, but acknowledging that something is happening and that we need to get out of here. He rounds the side of the jeep and pops open the gas compartment, immediately beginning to fuel the jeep as fast as he can with as little noise as possible.

Behind him I see something staring back at me from the shadows of a large fern bush. It looks like a rooster's face, but it's bigger than any rooster you might find on a farm. *A cockatrice.* The blood red comb atop its head is spiked, almost like a triceratops, and its golden razor-sharp beak drips black venom, which they're known to secrete. Its eyes glow a phosphorescent pale blue. For an instant, its gaze meets mine and I feel my blood run cold. Then, its eyes shift to Mr. Zeckel who is standing still, looking straight at me, very aware that there is something behind him. The creature inches forward, rocking from side to side, preparing to lunge. No time left to stay quiet.

"Mr. Zeckel!" I yell, reaching over Janice. The beast lunges out of the bushes. "MOVE!" I yell. Mr. Zeckel ducks to the side, dropping the gas. The cockatrice misses him and head-butts the car instead.

Janice screams as the window next to her cracks under the force of the blow, splintering in concentric circles like a spider web.

"Everyone hold on!" yells Mr. Zeckel, jumping into the car, throwing the key in the ignition and stepping on the gas all at once. He doesn't even bother to close his door, but the force of the car launching forward swings it shut. "Thanks for the assist Mr. Lau." He nods at me in the rearview mirror.

"No problem," I say, still shaking. I turn to look out the back, and to my horror, three of the birds are chasing us. They're as tall as any of us, these roosters of death. Their muscular bodies are a dark muddy-brown except for their wings and tail feathers which are a deep forest green.

Their talons dig into the ground as they propel forward at an unreal speed. The jeep is flying down the pavement at over 60 miles per hour, yet these birds are actually managing to keep up. Even worse, they're catching up to us.

"What are they, Henry?" asks Zach. He knows I know. And he knows I wouldn't be terrified if I thought they were friendly like the gryphons.

"Cockatrices," I say. "Three of them."

"What do they do?" asks Erika. "They look like gangster chickens!"

"*Mythological* versions could paralyze you just by making eye contact," I say. This alone is enough to send shivers down my spine. Eye contact has always been hard for me, so the thought of a creature that kills you with it is literally the stuff of nightmares.

"And *real* versions?" asks Noah.

"Um," I say, trying to curb my fear enough to think. "Okay, so sort of similar. Looking them in the eye can cause you overwhelming fear. Sometimes even to the point of being unable to move or think. They're also super poisonous." I look up at the others who are all staring at me. I try to not meet any of their gazes but it's so hard and I'm shaking and, holy shit, I'm crying. Actual tears are sliding down my face. "Fuck!" I'm so overwhelmed with terror that I can't help but to curse out loud.

"What's going on, Henry?" asks Erika.

"I looked it in the eyes," I say, sobbing. "When I saw it behind Mr. Zeckel. Only for a second but I ... Oh God!" I'm gasping for air, shivering and totally freaking out.

"Henry," says Erika. She's turned so she's wedged in the space between where our seat ends, and the back of the front seat begins. She looks right at me and takes my hands, squeezing them in hers. "You have to calm down, hun. Come on. You can do this. Just breathe."

"I can't!" I scream. "I can't breathe!"

"We're almost back to the Palace kiddo," says Mr. Zeckel. "I can see the spires from here. Just a little further and we'll be safe."

"We won't be," I cry. "We won't ever be safe. There'll always be a cockatrice, or a dragon, or some messed up kid who brings a gun to school, or a driver who ignores a stop sign. There is always going to be some horrible thing around every corner. Life is just us running away from death until it finally catches us!"

Erika is at a loss for words and lets go. I'm losing it. I'm losing my shit. Everything is so fucking scary, I don't ever want to leave this jeep. I don't want to ever move ever again, because I'll die. I know it. I *feel* it.

"Henry!" Noah cups my face in his hands and turns me so that my eyes meet his. "Hey. Henry. Look at me. You can beat this. Listen to my voice. You. Can. Beat. This."

"I can't," I sob uncontrollably. My face is wet with tears at this point and my body is drenched in sweat.

"Everything isn't scary. You know that. Some things are, sure, but there is good in the world. The unicorn was good. You felt it. Think about that. And that dragon? *You* helped it. You saved it. Henry, the world is not a horrible terrible place. It can't be. You know how I know?"

I shake my head, taking short, painful breaths through my nose.

I know, because of you." Noah is crying too now. He wipes the tears away and then refocuses on me. "When my . . . when Matthew died, I didn't wanna go outside either. I was so fucking scared. But I'm so glad I did. I'm so happy I got myself out of my room and my sadness because I met you. I was a jerk in the beginning. I was scared. Scared to actually like someone again. And then you helped me to remember how good the world can be. The world is only as dark as you make it. And you, Henry, you make the world a brighter place to be. I believe there is good in this world because I believe in you. And you can fucking beat this."

He continues to stare into my eyes as a single tear rolls down his cheek. His hands feel so warm against my face. So safe. My eyes pinch closed and then open again. I take what feels like the deepest breath I've ever taken in my life. My heartbeat slowly returns to normal and my body unclenches as I stop shaking.

"Okay," I say.

"Okay," he says, like a reassuring echo.

"Okay," I repeat.

"You're okay," he says. I feel his thumbs caressing my cheeks.

"I'm okay."

SLAM! One of the cockatrices throws its entire body into the side of the jeep. We're all tossed sideways in our seats as Mr. Zeckel does his best to keep the jeep from losing control.

"Gas is on empty!" yells Zach from the front, eyeing the jeep's dashboard.

"They must have busted the gas tank when they hit the jeep," says Mr. Zeckel. "Don't worry. We'll make it!"

"We're running on fumes!" cries Zach.

"We'll make it!" Mr. Zeckel bellows, his knuckles white as he grips the steering wheel.

Another cockatrice slams into the jeep on the front left side and the whole vehicle swerves right. Mr. Zeckel pulls on the wheel with all he's got, but it isn't enough. I feel the world tip as we flip sideways. The jeep slams onto its side, then continues rolling down a hill, bouncing off of tree trunks along the way. We hold on for dear life, our seatbelts straining to keep us in place. The two glass windows in the front shatter, one by one. The front windshield holds out as long as possible but finally cracks and then tears itself from the jeep altogether. Everyone screams as we flip over and over again, tossed in every direction a person can be tossed.

I think we break the tree line of the hill because light floods through the windows on all sides. I try to focus outside to see where we are which only serves to make me more nauseous. The jeep explodes through a brick wall into a large building, crashes across a tile floor, pushing several chairs and tables out of the way, and finally slows. We tip once more into an upright position. Stopping at last.

We take several deep gasping breaths. Even though we've physically stopped moving, the world around us is still spinning. I feel so dizzy I might throw up. Judging by the brown goo on the back of Mr. Zeckel's seat, Janice *has* thrown up. She wipes her mouth ashamedly.

"Everyone okay?" asks Mr. Zeckel. He turns to look at us and I can see that a thin line of blood is running down his face from a cut on his forehead.

We all moan.

Thomas opens the door and throws his head out, heaving his stomach onto the floor. I shift my gaze outside of the jeep to try and determine where we've landed. We're inside a store of some kind. The smell hits me all at once. Cookies. We've landed in a bakery, and to my knowledge there is only one bakery in Mythos.

"Are we . . ." asks Erika, who also must recognize where we are.

"The bakery in Town Square," I say. "We made it." Mr. Zeckel pushes open his door and gets out of the jeep, followed by Zach who I'm guessing has no desire to crawl over Thomas' puke.

Noah and Janice open their doors and we all get out of the jeep, stepping on broken glass and debris as we go. The store is dark except for the light outside and as far as I can tell, it's totally abandoned.

I go to the front window of the bakery which is also inexplicably shattered. I carefully poke my head out and look up and down the street. There's no one in sight. It's as if we've stumbled onto some terrifying ghost version of Town Square. The buildings all look as though they've been looted and ransacked. The street is filled with discarded bags, trash and merchandise.

"What happened here?" I say under my breath. But even as I ask the question, I'm not entirely sure I want to know.

I turn to see Janice moving towards the back of the shop, looking up and out of the hole the jeep has created in the rear wall. Suddenly, her face fills with terror as she points up through the hole. "They're coming down the hill!" she yells.

I turn back to look down the fake cobblestone path outside, and there, at the end of the street, stands the Palace. Its large doors are open, and even though the lights inside are off, I somehow know that getting to that castle is our one and only shot at surviving this hell. Our one and only shot at safety.

"We have to run," I say. Everyone turns to look at me. "We can make it to the Palace, but we have to go now!"

No one argues. We all leap through the window, careful not to cut ourselves on the shards of glass still remaining around the frame and start down the faux cobblestone street towards the Palace, running as fast as we can. Mr. Zeckel is the last one out the window. I hear him curse behind me and I look over my shoulder to see him ripping the leg of his pants free of the glass, which has snagged him and held him back. He isn't stuck long, but that one second gives the cockatrices extra time to catch up to him. As he runs, one of the birds, now on the roof of the bakery, flaps its wings, swoops down and lands on top of Mr. Zeckel, knocking him off his feet.

He cries out as he's slammed face first onto the ground.

I stop in my tracks, looking back helplessly. The bird pecks the ground, nearly hitting our teacher as he squirms and rolls from side to side.

"Keep your eyes closed!" I yell. As if that will help. The cockatrice is seconds away from stabbing him to death with its razor beak. If he closes his eyes now, he's definitely done for.

Zach sprints past me, heading for the rooster and Mr. Zeckel.

"Zach!" I yell, but he doesn't stop. He grabs the dragon tooth from around his neck and yanks it free. He reaches the cockatrice and lifts the tooth over his head before mercilessly bringing it down into the cockatrice's skull. The bird scrambles to the side, screaming in pain. Zach helps Mr. Zeckel up and together they start running towards me.

"I told you that thing was cool," says Mr. Zeckel.

"Thing was ugly as hell but if wearing it for two days is the price for keeping you from getting eaten by a death rooster, I'll pay it," says Zach.

"Come on!" yells Noah, grabbing me by the arm and pulling me along towards the Palace. We run together, side by side towards the castle doors. Janice, Erika and Thomas are ahead of us. Zach and Mr. Zeckel are behind us. I can hear the other two cockatrices behind us too, clucking and cawing angrily as they home in on their prey.

"Don't stop!" yells Zach. "They're right behind us!"

We reach the bridge as Janice, Thomas and Erika head through the double doors. They each grab hold of the doors, ready to pull them closed the moment we're inside. Noah and I get there next and we turn to see Zach and Mr. Zeckel just starting to cross the bridge. The cockatrices are nearly on them and I watch in horror as one leaps to the other side of the bridge, turning around, ready to pounce. Mr. Zeckel reaches into his pants pocket, pulling out a bright red flare gun. Several small shells are attached to the back of the gun by a black clip. He shoves Zach forward past the cockatrice and confronts it, taking the attention off of Zach. The bird lunges towards Mr. Zeckel, cawing as if it's just seen first light. Mr. Zeckel points the flare gun at the bird and pulls the trigger.

A blinding flash of light erupts from the flare gun and slams into the rooster's chest. In a daze and off-balance, it falls over the side and into the river. Mr. Zeckel runs inside and together we all pull on the doors. Through the space between the doors as they close, we see the last cockatrice charging and no sooner do the two doors meet, do they shudder from the impact of the cockatrice slamming into them from the outside.

Mr. Zeckel turns the giant lock on the door, and we all step back. The door continues to shake as the cockatrice tries desperately to get inside, but for the time being, it seems that we're safe.

"We did it," I say, a smile creeping onto my face. "We made it back . . . alive! You guys, we did it!" I look at each of them and we all smile at each other as we struggle to catch our breaths. After everything we've been through, we've finally made it back. All of us. *Alive.*

"Henry!" The voice comes from behind and I turn to see a familiar face walking towards us from the central aisle in the middle of the darkened store.

I smile because despite all the complications between Noah and I, I'm still super happy to see him. My smile broadens across my face as I call joyously back. "Vincent!"

THIRTEEN

Considering how beat up, bruised and broken all of us look, Vincent looks almost pristine. In fact, he looks exactly like when I last saw him three days ago. I run up and throw my arms around him. Seeing him, touching him, it all feels so right. Like a cup of coffee on a Monday morning. I'm so relieved to be near him again I could cry. He hugs me back as I bury my face in his chest. It's the first time I've really noticed how much taller than me he is.

It's the first time I've noticed a lot of things actually. How good he smells. How thin he is. How cold his hands are. My mom has this thing where her hands are always icy to the touch. I realize now that Vincent is the same way, which I guess is good because maybe that will give him and my mom something to talk about when they finally meet. And oh my God, now I'm thinking about Vincent meeting my parents!

"I thought you were dead," I say into him.

"I'm fine, Henry. No need to worry." He pulls back but keeps his hands on my shoulders as he looks me up and down. "You look like you've been through hell."

"We have. We all have," I say. Vincent, however does not look like he's been through anything. He's wearing a tight black cardigan which drapes just past his waist, over a thin white shirt and black jeans. He's foregone his flip flops and is now completely barefoot. Perhaps standing on the cold floor with no shoes is what has made him so cold to the touch. "We figured you decided on the late tour."

"I did," he says. "I had other plans for the morning."

"That's good," I say. "Honestly, I think most of the people on the train didn't make it. It was horrible."

"But that's over now," he says calmly. He gently pushes a lock of my hair behind my ear with his finger. "And we're together. Just as it should have been from the start." This causes me to pause, because it's such a weird thing for him to say. "Oh, Henry. I'm just so happy you're here. After all, you made all of this possible. It would seem wrong for you to miss it."

"All . . . of what?" I ask. I take a step back, pulling free of his hands. There's a strange knot forming in the pit of my stomach. Something is definitely not right here. I step back again, moving away from this boy who I've been looking forward to seeing again. This boy who's consumed my thoughts the past two days. Now, suddenly, I don't want to be within arm's length of him.

"Everything," he says. "Without you, I never would have gotten in here. I never would have been able to stop this . . . place from hurting anyone else. I never would have been able to stop *him*. You were the key. You made my dreams come true." He shakes his head as if shaking away bad thoughts. "And I've been dreaming for such a long time."

"Guys?" I say, hoping that they're all waiting behind me, ready to back me up. I don't know why I feel like a fight is coming. After all, this is Vincent. Not some evil boss monster at the end of a dungeon. *Vincent.* Wonderful, kind, beautiful Vincent.

"Oh, about that," says Vincent with a shy smile. "Well, it's just that your friends weren't invited."

My blood runs cold as I turn around to see that all of the others are no longer standing behind me, but above me, pinned to the upper wall of the store above the door by some invisible force.

"Henry, run!" gasps Erika.

They're all struggling against whatever's locked them in place and yelling down at me. I can't help but wonder if they've been yelling at me this whole time and I just haven't been able to hear it. *"Go! Save yourself! Run! Get out!"*

I turn back to Vincent, my fists clenched. "Let them go!"

"Or what?" asks Vincent. "You'll fight me? Come on, Henry. We both know that won't end well for you. You're not a fighter. Better to just forget about them and join me. You can be my prince and we can rule over Mythos together. You *love* Mythos."

"I . . ." I start, feeling both betrayed and terrified at the same time. "Who even are you?" I ask. "*What* are you?" I add, because I suddenly realize I know very little about Vincent. He's holding my friends against the wall without even touching them. *How?* Is he a magical being? Does actual magic exist? Is any of this even possible? My thoughts whirl, as if attacking me. If Vincent is a magical being, does that mean he's a product of Mythos? Manufactured here as one of the attractions? But that's not possible! He looks like a normal human being. He has thoughts and feelings and a fashion sense for God's sake. Everyone knows that Mythos doesn't deal in intelligent beings. He can't be one of the mythical creatures. He can't! And yet . . .

"What am I?" He smirks. "Isn't it obvious? I'm the new ruler of Mythos."

"I mean," I gulp. "What sort of creature are you?"

He sighs. "The answer to your question is . . . complicated. Maybe we could talk about it over dinner?"

"Are you asking me out right now?" I snap. "Because

I do not appreciate that. Especially considering that you're apparently super evil."

"Oh, who isn't?" he asks. "Everyone's just out for their own self-satisfaction. You didn't care what I was before when I was fawning over you. All you cared about was that someone liked you. You were so desperate to be loved by someone, anyone. I could smell it on you. You stank of insecurity and loneliness. That was how I knew you'd be the one to help me."

"You don't know anything about me!" My voice shakes, because despite my anger, I think he actually might be right. And it's horrifying to think that he's somehow figured out my deepest, darkest fear. Worse yet, he's exploited it. I'll love anyone as long as they love me first. He's right. I'm so desperate to be with someone that I literally ran into the arms of this creature standing before me.

"Oh Henry. Let's not start off like this. Let's not be one of those dramatic couples." He actually laughs, because to him, this is all just some silly lover's spat. He actually thinks this is going to end with me going with him and becoming his prince, or whatever. "Let's just skip to the part where there's just us, and only us, for all eternity." He offers his hand to me. It's like I'm living in a warped version of *Dear Evan Hansen*.

"Don't!" Yells Noah from above me. I look up at him to see that he's shaking his head. "Don't you dare go with him!"

"Don't worry," I say turning back to Vincent. "I have no intention of going anywhere with you. Now let them go."

"No."

"You're a monster!"

"I'm a monster?" he asks. "Me? No. I'm not a monster. The people who built this place are monsters. The people who made me are monsters. The people who kept me trapped like some experiment are monsters. Dawson Saks is a monster! As far as I'm concerned, he's the most horrifying monster on this island."

"Dawson Saks changed the world," I say. "He's made dreams come true."

"And Nightmares too!" Vincent takes a deep breath. "Perhaps it would be easier to show you." He extends his hand to me once more.

"I already told you, I'm not going anywhere with you," I say.

"Sorry, but I wasn't offering you a choice." My whole body suddenly lurches forward as I fly towards Vincent, my feet skidding along the floor. When I reach him, he wraps the fingers of his outstretched hand in my shirt, balling up the fabric and holding me in place. He raises the other hand over my face and places his thumb on my forehead. There's a blinding white light. And then I wake up.

FOURTEEN

I gasp, struggling to inhale my first breaths. I sit up and try to get my bearings as my eyes adjust. Everything's blurry, but the world around me slowly comes into focus. It's fairly dark, with only sparse fluorescent bulbs in the ceiling above me. They seem to create more shadows than actual light. I'm lying in some sort of glass bed filled with yellow liquid. My arms and legs, which are all pale, have wires and tubes attached to them which extend until they disappear through small holes in the side of my bed, or pod, or whatever this is.

Around me, the room is filled with tall cabinets, desks and chairs. Machines whir, beep and hiss. There's no one in sight. I look down at myself. I'm naked except for a tight pair of silver-colored underwear. The reflective shorts hug my upper thighs and pelvis tightly. I hold up my hands in front of my eyes, closing them into fists and then opening them again. A thick silver ring hugs my middle finger. I try to pull it off but can't. I'm struck by the realization that this is the first time I've ever done any of this. Even though I understand the world around me as if I've lived in it before, I also know intuitively that I've just been born. Everything is both old and new all at once.

I reach to the tubes in my arms and pull them free, leaving dark marks in the skin where they were inserted. I do the same for my legs. Then I clumsily pull myself over the side of the glass bed, slipping out of the yellow liquid, and placing my feet on the tile floor. It's freezing cold, but the feeling of cold is comforting like an old friend embracing me after a long time away.

I turn to look at the bed, which looks more like a life support pod from the outside. It's long and oval shaped, and for some reason, it makes me think of a coffin. I run my fingers along the glass as I follow it to a small digital screen which is inlaid near where my head lay only moments ago. I read it to myself, and I get the distinct feeling that this is the first time I've ever 'read' anything. Even so, the words come to me as if I had retained the ability from a previous life.

Project: v1 Nc3 N-T.

Days in incubation: 293

Subject Species: Vampire

Species Attempt: 13

I turn as footsteps echo in the hallway beyond the room. A man walks past the doorway wearing a long-sleeved shirt, slacks and brown suede shoes. He doesn't notice me. I look down at myself, realizing maybe I should be clothed.

At the far rear end of the room, near a messy desk, I see a row of lockers. I go to one and open it. Nothing. I walk to the next one and open it as well. Inside, there is a white shirt, made of light fabric, and black jeans. A name tag hangs in the locker which reads 'Lauren Ravs.' This is a woman's locker, but it's all the same to me. I pull the shirt over my head and the pants onto my legs. They're tight, but I like the way they feel; like they're holding me together. As if I might fall apart at any moment.

I turn back towards the hallway and make my way out of the room. The longer I'm alive, the more questions I have. Who am I? How did I get here? What is my purpose?

The hallway is just as dark as the lab. I move into the first room I find. There is also no one here. Rather, the room is filled with three desks which all face a wall of water, literally a water tank built into one side of the room. I peer into the murky depths and see several large creatures dart by.

Their front halves are moss-green horses with blood-red eyes. But they have no hind quarters or legs. Instead, the entire back half of their bodies are made up of a kind of seaweed which ripples through the water as they swim, propelling them forward. They come right up to the glass, neigh at me, then bolt off, disappearing from sight.

After watching them for a time, I leave the room and proceed to the next. Here I find another lab and another creature, but where the horse creatures seemed to be peacefully enjoying the day, this one looks as if it has been made to suffer.

The creature, only half my height, has the head of an elk, with large antlers protruding from atop it. Its face looks as though it's covered in blood and its teeth are sharp and canine. The creature stands on two legs. On its chest, where there should be skin and flesh, muscles and bones are exposed. It has two long arms which reach all the way to the ground, each ending in clawed paws. The lower half of its body is like that of a goat with thick haunches and hooved feet. The creature is horrifying to behold but the treatment it's enduring is even worse.

It's been chained to the wall and left with several tubes and wires inserted into it from all sides. It takes deep labored breaths, staring at me in fear as I enter the room. I feel as though I could weep simply at the sight of this beautiful animal made to exist in a constant state of indignity.

It's too much for me to bear. I turn and leave the room, hoping to catch my breath before finding a way to free the animal. The second I exit I'm met with cold steel placed on my right temple, immediately followed by the sound of a gun cocking, stopping me in my tracks.

"Honestly Richard, there's no need for that," says a female voice. A middle-aged woman with black hair steps in front of me and uses her bony hand to grab and lower the barrel of the gun placed on my temple. She then shoos the soldier, Richard, away. She turns to me and smiles, adjusting her blouse, skirt and name badge, which reads *Patricia.* "Sorry about that. You woke up a little earlier than expected. Gave us a startle. But it's alright now. I'm here to take you to see Mr. Saks."

"Mr. Saks?" I'm hearing my voice for the first time. It's so strange and foreign on my tongue.

"Yes. Your creator. He's very excited to meet you. Come along." She starts down the corridor and I follow. Richard, the soldier, follows close behind. I know because I can hear his combat boots stomping along the floor, just waiting for me to stop so that he can use the piece of weaponry cradled in his arms.

Following Patricia through the long halls, corners, and doors makes me feel as if I'm being led through some sort of labyrinth. I make a mental note of everything I see. The last two doors require Patricia to swipe a keycard in order to gain entry. After all the endless winding, we finally come to an elevator. Patricia ushers me on, leaving Richard behind. He grumbles but doesn't follow us. We go up to the very top floor and when the doors open, I'm greeted by a beautiful office that is not only enormous, but also looks out through a fully windowed wall over a vast landscape filled with lush forests, lakes, rivers and mountains. Beyond the land, I can see a deep blue ocean surrounding everything.

"Mr. Saks," says Patricia. "I've brought the new vampire as you requested."

The elevator doors remain open, as I stare out, transfixed by the view. The floor is marble and every piece of furniture, be it a sofa or a wide desk, is a pristine white. I notice a man standing to the right side of the room, leaning on the back of a sofa as he stares out the window, down towards what appears to be a large amphitheater about halfway through construction.

Mr. Saks turns to look at us and grins. He has an incredibly handsome face and a fit physique. He wears a blue V-neck long-sleeved shirt and black slacks, along with polished black shoes. He moves towards me, passing a coffee table and his desk which holds three curved computer monitors. He reaches out his hand and I instinctively go to take it. But where my hand should cross the threshold into the room and out of the elevator, it is stopped. There's a crackling sizzle in the air around my fingers and my hand retracts from the pain. There seems to be an invisible barrier between myself and the room.

"Ow," I say, looking at my fingers to see if any damage was done. They look perfectly normal. Then again, I have a feeling that what passes as normal for me doesn't apply to others.

"Oh, I almost forgot," says Saks. "Subject v1 Nc3 N-T, please come in." I look at Patricia, because now this feels like some sort of trap. She smiles and nods. I step forward, and this time I move into the room easily. No barrier. No resistance. No sizzle.

"Aha!" shouts Saks, as if this is some sort of victory for him. "You can't imagine how much of a headache that little trick has caused us. Here's hoping we got it right this time." He takes my hand in his, and we shake. I immediately want to pull away. His skin is far too warm.

"Please call me Dawson," he says, pulling away. "After all, we're practically family."

I nod as he turns and offers me a seat on the sofa. I follow him and sit on one end, while he sits on the other. He crosses his legs and stares at me. I can't help but notice that Patricia is still standing just outside the elevator. Perhaps she too requires some sort of invite in order to sit, or else the sofa might eat her.

"Look at you," says Dawson who eyes me up and down. "You really are a marvel. The best one yet, wouldn't you say Patricia?" I turn to see Patricia nodding once more. "Let me ask you, do you know who you are? Or rather, do you know *what* you are?" He stares at me, ready to analyze my answer.

"I . . ." I start, because no matter who or what you are, it's not an easy question to answer. "I am . . . alive."

Dawson smiles. "That you are. But there's more to it than that. See, here at Mythos we're building a park with attractions unlike anything the world has ever seen. A park built on the idea that any mythological creature you imagine can be real. By taking the scientific power of genetics and blending it with a little bit of magic, we've been able to create beings that have never once existed until now. In short, we make fantasy into reality." He smiles proudly at this.

He reaches over to the coffee table and picks up a tablet computer. On the screen I can see a pie chart and several lines of numbers. "Polls indicate that the top three creatures people want to see are dragons, unicorns and you. *Vampires*. Leave it to pop culture to shift the public consensus." He tosses the tablet back to the table. "You are going to make so many people so happy when they get to see you. Not to mention how excited we are to start figuring out your talents. After all, many of the creatures we've created here have yielded ... very unexpected results, given their mythological counterparts. For example, no one could have predicted that Krakens ate mainly wood. Well, that and *fear*. That was a surprise indeed. Though, I suppose many of our creations have deep ties to human emotions." He raises his eyebrows excitedly at me. "Of course, we like to keep that hush hush. Market research shows that people don't like the idea of animals which can eat their emotions. They start getting ideas of secret government conspiracy theories, and no one needs that on their plate." He shudders at the thought.

"Sorry, I got off track," he says with a dashing smile. "We were talking about you. Once we figure out how you actually work, your abilities and such, we'll develop a whole area for you, with rides and attractions. Maybe even a meet a greet. I can see you being a very popular photo op with young ladies. Mark my words, you will be a headlining feature of this park."

I look at him hoping to find something he's saying that makes me feel as excited about this prospect as he seems to be. But I can't figure out what that is yet. I think of the creature chained to the wall several floors below us and wonder if it too will be a 'headlining feature.'

"But we're getting ahead of ourselves. First thing's first. Let me take a look at those pearly whites of yours." He moves closer on the couch so that he's sitting right in front of me.

"Pearly whites?" I ask.

"Your teeth, of course," he says, then looks at Patricia. "Not enough to make a vampire from scratch. It's also gotta look like one, am I right?"

"You are right, Mr. Saks," she says.

I hesitantly part my lips so that Dawson can look at my teeth. He peers into my mouth. I'm hoping to see more excitement on his face. I don't know why, but it makes me feel good to please this person I've just met. But instead, he looks as though he's a balloon that's just been deflated.

"Oh damn," says Dawson. He looks up at Patricia. "No fangs."

Patricia walks over to look at my teeth, which are still showing. "Are you sure?" she asks.

"Of course, I'm sure, Patricia!" Dawson snaps at her. I see her recoil like an animal which has just been hit.

Dawson gives me another smile, but this one seems

fake. "It's been a big day for you already, what with being born and all. Why don't I have my assistant show you to your room?" He looks at Patricia who nods vigorously and then takes me by the arm, helping me to my feet. As we walk, I reach up and feel my teeth with my fingers. He's right. No fangs. Am I meant to have had them? I don't feel any worse for not having them. What does their absence mean for me? What does it mean for Dawson Saks?

We get back in the elevator. Patricia presses a button and swipes her keycard. As the doors close, I just barely catch a glimpse of Dawson as he walks to the window overlooking the park and punches the glass.

We descend several floors and emerge into a dimly lit hallway lined with thick solid white walls inlaid with a row of doors on either side. She takes me to the third one on the right, fishes a key from her pocket and places it into the lock. The door swings open to reveal a small cube shaped room. There's a cot in the back of the room and a metal chair in the dead center. A small black screen is fixed near the ceiling on the rear wall, tilted downwards. Perhaps I will be permitted to watch it. There are also small vents in the wall.

I enter the room, and no sooner am I inside, does the door close and lock behind me. I move to the door and

233

place my hand on its white surface. It's cold to the touch, and even though it's only a door, the cold makes it more comforting than holding Dawson's hand. I go to the center of the room and sit down in the chair. I look up at the screen, wishing that something would appear on it.

Nothing does. Instead, billowing flames burst from the vents in the walls and fill the room on all sides, burning me alive.

I feel my skin melt and boil as I fall to the floor, screaming in agony, hoping that my short life will end so that I no longer have to endure this hell. I burn and burn and burn. But I don't die. I feel every second of my body melting at the hands of the fire, but I survive. When the flames dissipate, I lay on the floor, a charred husk. Eventually, I feel the tiny threads of life within me stir as my body weaves itself back together. I'm not sure how much time passes but eventually, my body repairs itself.

When my legs have sewn themselves back together, I stand and move back to the chair. There I sit as my body continues to heal. The moment I feel completely whole again, the screen above me comes to life and I see the perfect image of Dawson Saks staring back at me. There's a smile on his face, but I don't think it's one born of happiness or joy.

"Well, well, well," he says. "This is a new

development. All of the prior versions of you died by fire. Which honestly, given the way we built you, was quite disappointing."

"Let me go," I say. Something about surviving certain death has made me feel bolder. "I'm not good enough for you, and you can't kill me. So just let me go."

Dawson laughs. Actually laughs. "Let you go? Where? You're not a person. You don't have anywhere *to* go. You're a failed theme park attraction." The words fall like a blow to my chest. I grit my teeth. My teeth that aren't good enough to allow me to live. I understand now. I'm just an experiment. A failed experiment.

"But not to worry," continues Dawson. "We're not surprised by your sudden immunity to fire. *Regular* fire anyway. I suppose it's not so much an immunity as it is a regeneration. We've planned for this. It's all just happening a little ahead of schedule. And let me tell you, in this business, I believe ahead of schedule is a blessing in disguise no matter where it comes from." He chuckles to himself. "We'll observe you, for now. See if any more powers develop. But rest assured, we will find a way to destroy you." He smiles. "Have a good day. In fact, have several. After all, you only have so many left. Of that, you can be certain." The screen goes black.

I live through the day. I live through several. Every

day I keep expecting the walls to fill the room with fire or some other form of torture, but for a time, none comes. As the days pass, I start to learn things. I learn that if I focus hard enough, I can make the lights in the room go out. Of course, the first time I succeed at this, the room fills with fire and burns me to a blackened crisp again. It takes me several hours to return to my regular self. Less time than before. The pain is horrendous, but in time, I've learned to accept pain as part of my existence.

I further discover that if I focus my ears, I can hear voices and sounds far beyond the room I'm in. Mostly I just hear scientists talking about their day to day lives and what they miss from back home. Their wives, husbands, families and children. Humans, it turns out, are incredibly interesting to listen to. They all have hopes and dreams, triumphs and failures, moments of unexpected joy and others of bottomless sorrow.

I'd like to have hopes and dreams someday. I think of the world I saw through Dawson's office window. I imagine myself looking out over the forests and valleys with a companion by my side. I think this is what the humans refer to as a daydream. But this one is mine and mine alone.

I start to lose track of time. I no longer know how many days have passed. My ears perk up one day when I hear Dawson's voice somewhere through the walls. He sounds angry as he speaks to Patricia, a voice I've become very familiar with.

"We're running out of time, Dawson. The park needs to open. We've pushed it back long enough. The investors are threatening to pull out."

"Not until the dragons are ready," he says angrily.

"The dragons *are* ready. You have to let it go. We can't keep wasting resources on them. It's one little thing. People are going to be thrilled just to *see* one. It won't matter that they can't breathe fire."

"It matters, Patricia," snaps Dawson. "Dragons breathe fire. It's the main thing people think about when they imagine them. I will not open this park until we've got a dragon who looks and acts the way people expect them to!"

"And how do you plan to make that happen? We don't have the children anymore, thanks to your friends in the media. And even if we did, it wouldn't make a damn difference. We only ever managed to make one living specimen, and it destroyed one of our facilities and killed three geneticists before the beast blew up!"

"They are not my friends."

"Obviously." She sighs. "We have to face the facts. Cut our losses."

There's a long moment of silence. Then Patricia continues to speak.

"Unless this isn't about wowing our guests at all."

"What are you implying?" growls Dawson.

"I'm implying that maybe the reason you're so hell bent on the dragons breathing fire is because of *him*." Silence again.

"He needs to be destroyed Patricia."

"Why, Dawson? He's locked away where no one will ever find him. Face it, this is about your ego. You just hate that he reminds you that once in a while, even the great Dawson Saks fails."

There's a loud noise like a clap. Skin against skin.

"The only thing that reminds me of my failure," says Dawson. "Is *you*. That's why I keep you around, Patricia. That's why I pay you more than God, so you never leave. Because looking at *you* reminds me that I almost sacrificed my career for you. All because I thought I was in love. Loving you enough to almost give up everything was my only failure. This thing with the vampire? This is merely an inconvenience." I hear steps which fade into the distance. Then I hear Patricia's small gasping breaths somewhere nearby as she sobs quietly by herself.

Moments later, Dawson takes out his rage on me. The room fills with fire, incinerating me yet again.

Days later, I begin to notice strange smells. At first, I wonder at their origin. It's only after they intensify that I realize that what I'm smelling are actually human emotions. Every time I breathe in, the feelings of the people near my cell flood my nostrils. Fear, exhaustion, hunger, joy, envy, love. I smell them the way a human might smell freshly baked bread. And I realize, to my surprise, that breathing in their emotions seems to fill me up. As if some hunger inside of me is being satiated.

My greatest discovery comes soon after. It starts when I begin experimenting with visualization. I find that if I visualize individual particles of myself, I can move them from one place to another with a simple thought. I can quite literally 'shift' myself through space. The first time I shift, it's only two inches to my left. I continue to practice this and pretty soon I can shift from one side of the room to the other. One second, I'm here, the next, I'm there. I do this several times in a row and just when I'm feeling very proud of myself, the screen above me comes on once more. Dawson glares down at me.

"Learned a new trick, have you?" he asks.

"I'm getting stronger," I say.

"To what end?" he asks smugly. "So you can impress everyone? Maybe perform at parties like a circus clown? No one cares about you. No one even knows you exist."

"You do," I say. "You know I exist. And you're here so you obviously care." I find myself smiling up at him because the look on his face says it all. *I'm right.*

"I tell you what I'm going to do. I'm going to press this button and I'm going to fill that room with fire. And then, I'm going to make sure the fire never stops. The rest of your potentially very long life will be spent burning. It will be my very favorite attraction here at Mythos. The Vampire in Hell. I'll visit it often."

"You are a bad man," I say.

"Only to you," he says. "The rest of the world loves me. I've brought joy to thousands, soon to be millions. The park is a success. No thanks to you. Critics are raving. Profits are beyond expectations. You're the only one with anything negative to say, and you don't even exist." He sighs, as if he's finally found some peace. "It's been a good run, but this is goodbye." He presses the button and the room begins to fill with fire. As the flames reach me, I close my eyes, focusing on shifting away from this place.

When I open my eyes, I'm no longer in the room. I'm not even inside. I spin around to see that I'm standing on a cobblestone street, lined with shops, and filled with people of all shapes and sizes. No one seems to have noticed me appear out of nowhere. It's mid-day and the sun feels warm on my skin. It doesn't burn me, but the warmth is severely uncomfortable. At the end of the street, I see a huge castle with towers which reach to the sky. I can't explain why, but I know that Dawson is there. It doesn't hurt that the way the building looks down on everyone below reminds me of him. His office must be located in one of those towers high above.

I focus on shifting once more and the next moment, I'm standing in front of the open double doors. I take a step forward amidst crowds of humans entering and leaving. But as my bare foot hits the threshold a yellow static crackles around my foot, forcing me to recoil. I try once more with my hands, but the same thing happens. I'm locked out, just like I was so long ago when I tried to enter Dawson's office without his permission.

I don't understand. I should be able to enter this place. I'm almost certain I've spent my whole life within its walls. Unless . . . perhaps this is another flaw in my design. Much like my teeth.

I back up and observe the doorway. A placard is inlaid into the stone just above it. "Here stands the Grand Palace. A gift from the lords and ladies of Mythos to all who travel here from across the sea." I don't have time for riddles. I focus on shifting through the barrier, hoping to end up on the other side. But though my body technically shifts, I simply reappear in the same spot as before.

There must be something I'm missing. Dawson invited me into his office. *His* office. Perhaps I need an invite through this door as well. But who owns this castle? *All who travel here from across the sea.*

Frustration flares in my chest. I take in a deep breath and the emotions of the humans all around me fill my nostrils. Anxiety and excitement, anticipation and worry. But one smell stands out from the rest. One smell hits me in a way I've never been hit before. It smells like desperation, but with a light seasoning of love. Someone wants so badly to be loved and accepted that it cuts like a knife through every other emotion. And that gives me an idea.

I turn and look through the crowd, sniffing the air. I shift down the street and sniff once more. He's close. Next to me is a small stand selling flip-flops on a rack. I take a pair and place them on my feet, hoping they will protect me from the warmth of the street. The shopkeeper shouts at me, but I sniff again and shift in the direction of the smell, leaving his deep voice far behind.

I'm now within some sort of moving compartment. Several young humans sit around me. They look about the same age as I appear. I guess I was made to look very young. I take a seat since most of them seem to be sitting. I scan the faces around me.

I see him sitting next to a dark-skinned girl. He has light brown skin and jet-black hair. Our eyes lock. The embers of a new ability smolder inside of me. I get the sense that I could hold power over this young man through the simple act of gazing into his eyes. I'll need to experiment with this theory of course, but I've yet to find a power I couldn't master. I smile at him, look around, then get up and move to sit next to him.

"Hey, I'm Erika," says the girl on his other side. She extends a hand and I shake it, despite not having shaken a hand since the day I met Dawson Saks. Was that days ago? Or years? I have no idea.

"Vincent," I say without hesitation. I suppose, in a way, it's been my name since the day I was born. Since the day I saw a version of that name on my birthing cell.

"You're one of the band kids, am I right?" she asks.

I nod. "Totally. How'd you know?" I don't even know what a band kid is.

"I'm psychic," she says and then winks. I don't know if she can actually read my mind, but I imagine she can't. Humans, in my experience, aren't capable of anything extraordinary. They're weak and riddled with flaws. The only thing they do well is *feel* and they do it so much I'd say it was more of a detriment than a power.

"She really is," says the boy. "She totally knew I was

gay before even I did," he says. He looks at me with affection as his face turns red.

"You're cute," I say. And I mean it. Already I'm imagining him next to me at the great window in Dawson's office, looking out over our little world together. He will be mine.

"This is Henry," says the girl. She then invites me to join them at the Kraken Amphitheater and the gift shop later. I accept. It's as if the universe is offering me a gift for all the torture I've endured.

As we leave the train, I see several clandestine armed guards approaching the cars with guns in hand. Richard leads them. He's put on weight since I first saw him holding a gun to my head on that first day. He should have killed me when he had the chance. I shift. Now I'm standing in front of a small store selling candy.

Did they track me here or is it just a coincidence? And if they did track me, how did they do it? I rack my brain as the heat of the sun presses down on me. I raise my hand to shield my eyes, and that's when I see it. The ring on my finger is blinking a faint red light. I try pulling the ring off, but it won't budge. Frustrated, I place the whole finger in my mouth and bite down just behind the ring. I barely feel the pain at this point. I spit the finger and ring out. The ring topples to the ground. The cut where my finger was doesn't even bleed. It's just a black stump and before I have time to examine it, a new finger grows in its place. It's almost ironic that my teeth, the reason for my imprisonment, have now become my salvation.

I shift near to the amphitheater and sit on a long bench, observing people as they pass by. I wait until Henry and Erika appear, heading for the theater. I follow them closely and right before the show starts, I take my seat next to Henry.

"For a minute there I thought I wouldn't be able to find you guys," I say, not wanting them to know I've been waiting. The lie tastes easy on my tongue and I think I understand why humans enjoy them so much.

"I knew you'd come through," says Erika.

"I'm glad you did," says Henry. "Find us, I mean." I put my hand on his leg and give it a gentle squeeze. My prince is warm to the touch, but I'm sure we can find some way to fix that.

After the show, we make our way down the main street until we get to the drawbridge leading into the castle. But as we cross, I realize that he hasn't invited me in yet. If my theory is correct, then what allowed me through the shield into Dawson's room was his invite. If I don't do something quick, I'll be locked out all over again. I need to find some way to recreate that moment here and now. I stop in my tracks and wait for him to notice me.

"Hey," he says. "You okay?"

"Sorry," I say, trying to think of a new lie to tell. "I just got a little freaked out."

I smell his emotions fill with confusion. "Freaked out?" he asks.

"I know I come on a little strong," I say. "I just . . . when I saw you on the train, I instantly liked you." This part is true. I smell his joy at me saying this. "I just don't want you to feel like you have to hang out with me. I know your friend has sort of been pushing you to. I think you're super cute, but if you want me to leave you guys alone, I'll go."

The moment of truth. "I'm sorry, Vincent," he says. "This is all just really new to me. I hope I didn't give you the wrong impression. I DO want to spend time with you. I think the fact that you came up to me on the train is amazing and brave. I could never do that if it were the other way around. I'd be too nervous."

"Yeah," I say. "I was nervous about that. Truth is, I still am." I am nervous, but not about Henry. I already know he'll be my prince. I'm nervous about Dawson. I'm nervous about being caught before I get to exact my revenge.

246

"Well," he says. "Don't be. I liked it. I like . . . you."

"Really?"

"Really."

"So," I say. "You want me to come into the Grand Palace with you?" I lock eyes with him once more, sealing the connection between us.

"Yes," he says. Then he comes up to me and takes my hand, pulling me with him. "I want you to come in here and look at shirts and hats and tell me I look good in all of them. I want you to take selfies with oversized plushies with me and buy tons of pre-wrapped snacks that we'll inevitably get sick on. Come with me."

"Okay," I say. He takes my hand and we enter the Palace. I'm in. Up until now, I've been taking chances as they come, but now I need a real plan. Unfortunately, I may already be out of time. I see Dawson walking across the room with Patricia and another man in tow. I shift.

I'm on the other side of the store now. I watch as Dawson speaks to Henry and then they disappear into a side door. Every fiber of my being wants to shift to follow him, but I can't. I won't. Killing Dawson Saks would be easy. Too easy. I need him to suffer the way that he's made me, and all of his other creations, suffer. I need to discover his personal version of burning to death over and over again.

Suddenly, I know what I have to do. It comes to me like some divine realization. I have to destroy his park. I need to end his legacy. I imagine the place where it all started. The lab underground where I awoke so long ago. I shift and I'm there. It looks almost exactly as it did then. A scientist looks up from his desk at me. Fear broils off of him and fills my nostrils but not for long. I shift behind him, grab his head and twist, breaking his neck. Humans are so very fragile. It's no wonder they care so much about their reputations and legacies. They only have so long to realize their dreams. Unlike me. My dreams, like myself, will live forever.

A small tablet lies on the desk. I pick it up and open a folder entitled: Creatures. I scroll until I find the folder marked: Vampire.

Several hours slip by as I read about all the abilities they tried to imbue me with. All the times they failed before me and disposed of my predecessors. All the times they killed living beings in the name of science. When I'm done reading about vampires, I read through other dossiers, learning about the many creatures on the island, some which now reside here for the entertainment of humans. Others, like me, never made it that far. It's horrifying to read, but I can't take my eyes away. Each new subject brings a story of despair followed by a trail of death. If I didn't hate Dawson Saks before, I certainly do now. A small digital clock on the desk reads 8AM when I finally throw the tablet back onto the desk, next to the dead scientist, and leave the room.

I head down the hallway. Most of the rooms are abandoned. The kelpies are no longer in their tank. In fact, the tank has been completely drained of water. The elk-faced wendigo is no longer chained to the wall. But as I explore the rooms, I eventually find a whole family of beautiful wendigos locked away in a long row of cages. There are six of them now. And they're much taller than before, not to mention more muscular and more monstrous. The result of Dawson's experiments no doubt.

The creatures look at me curiously. "Hello my friends," I say. They stare at me, making no sound. "How would you all like to help me destroy our creator?" I pause, because he doesn't deserve that title. "Or rather, our *enslaver*, Dawson Saks."

The creatures mule and neigh, which I take as a yes. I walk down the line of cages, waving my hand over the padlocks, bursting them open. The creatures move out of their cages and follow me back out into the hallway. We find an elevator and I wave a hand over the hand-print scanner. The red screen turns green, and the doors slide open. Inside, I press the button next to the words

"Control Level." It sounds like the perfect place to start. We ascend the Palace until the elevator stops and the doors slide open. Someone stands on the other side of the door, waiting to board.

Patricia gasps at the sight of me and the pack of wendigos. "Y-you . . ."

I walk right up to her and place my hand on her cheek. She's trembling. Her terror fills my nostrils. I stare into her eyes for a long moment before finally stepping away. The wendigos move off the elevator and stand aside as they glare down at her.

"Go," I say.

"Y-you aren't going to kill me?" she asks.

"You've suffered enough already," I say. "You don't deserve to die."

"And Dawson?"

"He does."

"He's a good man," she says. "Or . . . he was at one point."

"I won't tell you again, Patricia. Run. Get out of here and do not look back." She gulps and enters the elevator, pressing a button before the doors slide closed.

We continue down the hall towards a set of double doors. I hold out my palm to them and they explode off their hinges, flying into the room ahead which is filled with men and women seated at computer terminals. They all duck out of the way, screaming in terror. Standing at the far end of the circular room is Dawson himself. I spot him instantly. He turns, and our eyes meet. Without a word from me, the wendigos move into the room, attacking the computer technicians, feeding for the first time in who knows how long. The techs barely put up a fight. Not that they'd have much chance anyway. The wendigos' breath turns them to ice before they can even run away.

Dawson moves towards me with rage in his eyes. He pulls a small handgun from his waist, points it at me and empties the weapon, firing off the entire magazine. The bullets fly through me as if I weren't even there. I charge at him, but a recognizable cry of pain behind me stops me in my tracks.

I turn to see Patricia lying on the floor, blood spilling from the bullet wounds in her body onto the blue carpeted floor.

"Patricia!" yells Dawson.

Why? Why did this woman come back for this monster?

Dawson runs past me, crouches down next to her and cradles her in his arms. "I . . ." he tries to speak, but maybe for the first time in his life, Dawson Saks is at a loss for words.

"I . . . couldn't leave you to . . . die," she says. He cups her face in his hands as she closes her eyes and breathes her last.

Humans are so fragile.

"You did this," he says, his eyes raising from her face to mine.

"You pulled the trigger," I say.

"You should have died years ago, but you just had to keep on living and now she's dead." He stands and launches towards me, but I hold out my palm and throw him backwards. He cries out as his body slams into the wall. I pin him there.

"No," I say. "You killed her just like you killed so many of us in order to create this place. But your days of hurting others are over. You're not going to hurt me or anyone else ever again. We will be free of you. And you're going to watch your little world burn to the ground. As of now, the park is officially closed." I raise my hands above me, focusing on the electricity which pumps through the walls and out to the park beyond. Sparks explode from the computers and rain down from the lights above. I tap into every pen, every enclosure, every cage this island has to offer. I open them. All of them. I free the slaves of this place from their imprisonment. There's an explosion and then the power goes out. *All* the power goes out.

FIFTEEN

"NO!" I yell, waking from the nightmare that was and still is Vincent's life. The pain, the anger, the loss. I saw it all through his eyes. I pat my chest and my face with my hands, making sure I'm me again. Making sure I'm Henry.

"Welcome back," says a voice I recognize. Only now do I realize that I am in a completely different place than I was prior to the visions of Vincent's life. It's dark with only faint hints of light coming through a window from dull fluorescent bulbs on the ceiling of a hallway. I can barely see the area around me, but it doesn't take long to realize that I'm in a cage, one very similar to those where Vincent found the wendigos. In fact, I think they are the very same cages. A small amount of old hay is strewn about the cold cement floor. I move in the direction of the voice and find Zach leaning against the back wall of his cage eyeing me through the bars.

"Was that Henry?" asks Erika from somewhere past Zach's cell. "Is he okay?"

"Looks fine to me," says Zach.

"Oh, thank God," says Erika. I can't see her, but she sounds relieved.

"Does he know how to get out of here?" asks Janice from the darkness.

"He just woke up, Janice. Give him a second." Zach looks at me expectantly.

"How . . . did we get here?" I ask. My mouth and throat are so dry that it hurts to speak.

"After your boyfriend up there knocked you out, he had those deer-head guys bring us down here."

"The wendigos," I say, trying to piece everything together.

"Sure," says Zach. "Threw us all in these cages and left. Said he'd be back when you woke up. We tried to break the locks but gave up. It's no use."

"How long was I out?"

"Few hours at least," says Zach. "What did he . . . do to you?"

"He showed me his past. All the way from his birth to now. He's the reason the creatures got loose, and the power went out. He's trying to take over the park. He and Dawson Saks have this feud going on and . . . I don't think he's going to stop until he's destroyed everything. Oh, and he wants to make me his prince." I groan.

"Sounds . . . super creepy."

"This is all my fault," I say.

"Come on, dude. Don't be dramatic."

"It is, though! I invited him into the Grand Palace."

"So?"

"So he's a vampire! He can only enter places he's been invited."

"Oh." Understanding dawns on Zach's face.

"I basically gave him the keys to this place and said, 'have at it.' And all because I was so desperate for someone to like me. I just . . ." I take a deep breath. "I just wanted someone to care about me. I wanted it so much that I let the first guy who gave me any attention into my life without even a second thought as to whether or not he was good for me." I look up at Zach. "Sorry, you probably don't want to hear this."

"Why not?" he asks.

"I mean, you don't necessarily like that I'm gay. You've made that pretty clear."

Zach rolls his eyes. "Are you really that dumb?"

"Excuse me?"

"You actually think I was pissed at you for liking guys?"

I pause. "Well, yeah."

"I don't care who you like, Henry. You're my best friend. I wasn't pissed at you for being gay. I was pissed at

255

you for lying to me. Every time I asked you which girls you liked, you'd just say some names, but you didn't even like girls. When we were ten, we had that sleepover where we both promised we'd never keep anything from each other, and I kept my side of that promise. I told you about how I was struggling with telling my Dad that I didn't think I was a Christian. And you told me something about your Mom keeping old ketchup packets. What you *should* have been telling me was that you're gay. You had every opportunity to tell me the truth, and you just kept lying. I thought we were closer than that."

"No ... I..." What do I even say here? I move closer to the bars so that I can see him better. "I'm sorry, Zach. These things aren't always easy to talk about." I inhale and breathe out with my whole body. "I guess coming out is such a personal thing, I didn't even stop to think about the fact that I was lying to you. For a long time, I was telling those same lies to myself. I'm so sorry."

"I'm sorry too," he says. "For being such a dick. I've just been so pissed at my Mom and Dad for all the pressure they've been throwing at me about college applications and my shitty grades. I felt like a walking train wreck. And then you came out and ... it was a lot, you know?"

"I know." I reach through the bars separating us and

squeeze his shoulder. "How about after we survive this, we grab some iced coffees and have a rant-fest about all of it?"

"Deal," he places a hand on mine and squeezes it.

"Are you two gonna make out now?" asks Janice from one of the cells I can't see.

"Shut up, Janice," says Erika. "They're having a bro moment."

"Wait," I hear Thomas say. "Zach is a gay vampire? Is that what I just heard? Oh God . . . am I next?"

"Seriously, who invited this guy?" asks Noah.

Noah. My chest tightens just hearing his voice. It's a good thing that Zach and I are making up, because I'm pretty certain I'm on Noah's shit list at this point. Especially after the way I ran into Vincent's arms. Vincent's evil, murderous arms.

"That's not how it works, Mr. Ruiz," says Mr. Zeckel. "Zach is neither gay, nor a vampire and you can't catch it. Being gay, that is. I'm not entirely sure about the vampire part."

They're all here. Everyone's safe, for the time being.

Zach laughs "First thing's first. We need to get out of here and stop that guy."

"You can't," says a new voice. This one comes from behind me. I turn and move towards the opposite side of my cage, peering through the bars. There on the other side, sitting on the floor and looking like hell, is none other than Dawson Saks.

"Mr. Saks?" I ask. "What are you doing here?"

"The vampire, the one you call Vincent, threw me down here," he says.

"See?" says Thomas. "Someone *did* say vampire!"

"Failed attempt at one, anyway," says Dawson.

"No offense, but I think comments like that are the reason he's so pissed off," I offer.

"I suppose."

"He showed me everything," I say. "His birth. You trying to kill him. Patricia . . ." I wait for Dawson to react, but he stays quiet. It's as if he's been drained of his will to care. "He wasn't born a monster. You made him one."

"He was and is a failed experiment," snaps Dawson. "Nothing more or less. You keep thinking of him as a person, but that's just what he wants you to think. He needed you to care for him to get through the front door. And you played right into his hand."

I hate that he's right. I hate that I was so naïve. Most of all, I hate that I'm at least partially to blame for everything that's happened. "Maybe we can fix this," I offer. "Maybe we can stop him."

"If he showed you everything," Dawson continues,

"then you know you can't. Nothing can. He's the reason we stopped development on all humanoid projects and relegated ourselves to creatures that were more animal in nature. We decommissioned the rest but were never able to complete his."

"You mean getting a dragon to burn him to death?"

"Precisely." He looks up at the ceiling, as if trying to recall something lost long ago. "Every creature on Mythos is weak to another creature on Mythos. It allows us to maintain natural order; an ecosystem of checks and balances. But it was also our contingency plan should something like this ever happen. In the best-case scenario, the beasts would destroy each other. The dragons die if stabbed by a unicorn horn. The kappas crave fairy meat but eating one will poison them. The rocs automatically see the gryphons as a threat and will attack on site. And the cockatrice's stare causes the kraken's body to shrivel. It was an elegant circular food chain, until we got to dragons and vampires. Because dragons simply do not breathe fire. Despite our best efforts, there are just some facets of magic that our science simply couldn't get right. Regardless of how much anyone believed it. The whole world believes dragons breathe fire, and that still wasn't enough."

"That's the secret ingredient," I say, slowly putting the puzzle of Mythos together. "Belief. That's the little bit of magic you always talk about in your interviews."

"When I was in first grade," starts Saks, "my teacher asked the class to raise our hands if we thought Godzilla was real. I was one of the kids who raised their hand. I knew full well that he wasn't. My parents wouldn't dare let me believe in something so ridiculous. But I wanted to live in a world where he *could* be real. I wanted to live in a world where anything is possible if you believe in it hard enough." He shrugs. "Of course, our teacher set the record straight. Godzilla wasn't real. Neither was King Kong. Neither were dragons or unicorns or any of them."

"So, you did all this to prove your first-grade teacher wrong?" I ask.

He actually lets out a small laugh. "I guess I did a little bit."

"I still don't understand how you used people's beliefs to make these creatures," I say.

"I could regale you with all the scientific mumbo jumbo my biologists and chemists constantly prattle on about, but the simple truth is that this island is special. There's something about this place that makes that little spark of magic possible. If a person believes something with all their heart, it can be real here. Though obviously it takes a bit more than belief to make a magical creature. Otherwise we wouldn't need all the science and the labs and the tests. Belief is more like the catalyst; the spark that gives them life.

"One geneticist explained it to me in terms of baking a cake. When you bake a cake, you need all these ingredients. Flour and sugar and eggs. And you need quite a bit of each. But arguably the most important ingredient is the one you use the least of: baking soda. You throw all these big hitters into a big bowl and then you add just a pinch of baking soda. It's almost as if it's not even there. Yet, without it, the cake wouldn't rise in the oven. It would just fall flat.

"That pinch of something that makes everything else work together? All the DNA and the muscles and the bones. That's belief."

There's a long moment of silence while I adjust my understanding of all the creatures of Mythos, as well as our time here, in relation to this new information. I remember our time with the unicorn and how I fully believed that unicorns could heal a person just before I touched it and my hand was healed. "So, if all it takes is a person's belief, why experiment on kids?"

"We didn't—" he growls, but then his expression softens. "Oh, what's the point of lying anymore. I'm as good as dead anyway." He sighs. "Kids are more likely to truly believe in the extraordinary. Their minds are more open to it. Especially early on in the park's development when this all seemed like a crazy pseudo-science circus. Children were willing to believe what adults couldn't even fathom. In the beginning, they were the easiest source of the 'spark' we needed to create life. Of course, once the media got a whiff of what we were up to, they made sure to shut us down.

"It was for the best, really. We'd hit a wall with the children at that point, anyway. We'd overestimated them. Kids today don't believe in things as easily as they used to when I was young. And why would they? They're bombarded with information often with little to no credibility behind it. Their access to the internet, television, movies, video games, not to mention social media has taught them how the 'real' world works too quickly, demystifying everything. They're taught to question everything, and believe nothing. We're all being taught to lose our sense of wonder earlier in life in favor of science and logic so that we're prepared for the harsh reality of a cruel world."

"But they failed in shutting you down. So where did you get your belief from after that?" I ask, not sure I want to know more, but unable to put a plug on my curiosity.

"A few clinically diagnosed psychopaths here. A few occult enthusiasts and practitioners there. All willing to submit to scientific experimentation in return for huge sums of money, three meals a day and free health care. You'd be amazed what people will do for free food and drugs."

Just then, there's a heavy thud on the floor, then another. I look up towards the foggy windows on the wall opposite the cages. The shadowed outline of a wendigo slowly passes by.

"But none of them believed the way some of the children did," says Dawson hauntingly, watching the Wendigo pass. "Any adult with enough morphine in their system can dream up a unicorn. But all of our most terrifying creations were the work of children. Because the thing children know better than anyone is how to be afraid."

His words hold me in their grip. I swallow hard. It's not until I'm looking out the window at the wendigo's silhouette that a thought occurs to me. "Wait. How is there light out there?" I ask.

"The subbasement is on an emergency generator," says Dawson. "We weren't totally unprepared for something like this. Only mildly unprepared."

My mind races. If belief is so potent here, we should be able to use that to our advantage, right? After all, if belief can create life, maybe it can do other things as well.

All we need to do right now is get out of here. I stand up in my cell and move to the door. There's a large padlock holding it closed.

"I believe the padlock is unlocked," I say. Then I give a push on the door. No dice. The door is still locked. I hear Dawson chuckling behind me.

"You really think it's that easy?" he asks. "You can't just start believing something on the spot. Beliefs are ingrained into you. And the older you are, the more your beliefs are fixed firmly in reality. There's a nearly invisible line between what you know and what you believe you know. The fact that you know that the door is locked means that you can't just suddenly start believing otherwise."

"Here I thought Thomas liked the sound of his own voice," says Zach on the other side of me. "But this guy puts him to shame."

"I'm simply explaining what we discovered in testing," says Dawson.

"Did you know that unicorns can heal people?" I ask.

Dawson scoffs. "That's only in fairy tales, kid. And even if they could, they wouldn't be able to get you out of here."

But he's wrong. Unicorns *can* heal people. One healed me. I willed that into reality even though I knew that the ones on Mythos weren't able to do it. And if I could make that happen, then I can make this happen. I'm not saying Dawson is wrong. But maybe there's a loophole he doesn't know about.

So, I stare at the lock and begin to think out loud. "It's locked. I know that to be true. Nothing I believe can make it less locked. But . . . okay, maybe it's rusted on the inside. Maybe it's got weak hinges and springs. Maybe the key has passed through the insides of this lock a lot. Maybe, while locking in wendigos, the scientists were in such a rush to lock the door, that they ended up being too rough with the lock." I'm onto something now. I can feel it. "Maybe the contraptions and gears inside have become dull and loose with age. In fact, maybe the lock is so old, so worn down, so decrepit that it could become faulty and spring open at any moment. Even now."

There's an audible click as the lock pops open.

"Holy crap," I say in a whisper, because I don't want the monster on the other side of the wall to hear me.

Dawson stands and walks to the wall of his cage to look through the bars. His eyes go wide at the sight of the opened lock. "But . . . how?" he asks. "It's not . . . you can't just . . ."

"I believed," I say, still surprised that it actually worked. And like a dam breaking in my mind, I suddenly realize the answer. The one that Dawson was too set in his ways to know. If you can believe in something so much that it becomes reality here, then it must work in the other direction too. I open my mouth and the words come spilling out. "I know how to defeat Vincent."

SIXTEEN

I move as quietly as possible, reaching outside the cell, removing the open lock and then pushing the door open. It creaks slightly, but not enough to alert the wendigos. I don't even know how many are outside the room. I worry I'll have to 'believe' all the locks are unlocked, which I imagine won't be easy, but then I see a key ring hanging from the wall. I grab it and, starting with Dawson's cage, open all the locks one by one. Erika hugs me as she exits her cell. Mr. Zeckel pats me on the shoulder. Even though Saks should shoulder the blame for Vincent, I can't help but still feel that I played a part in all of this. After all, I did fall for his lies, and now we're here. Thomas and Janice avoid looking directly at me. I don't blame them.

The last cell on the far end is Noah. I open his cage and he walks right up to me. "Stop," he says in a low whisper.

"Stop what?"

"Stop blaming yourself for all of this. Don't let this make you feel like you're a bad person, or whatever," he says. I'm taken aback. The guilt must be written all over my face, because that's exactly what I've been thinking. I've been struggling with the fact that my need to be loved has essentially brought about the end of Mythos. My desperation has literally ended lives. I truly feel as though the fate of the world was placed on my shoulders. And I failed. I failed everyone.

"It's not your fault. There is no way you could have known all this would happen. He used you. If it wasn't you, it would've been someone else."

"Yeah," I say. "But I could have been more careful. I could've, maybe, asked him more questions. Got to know him more before I flipped head over heels." I shake my head. "I'm so stupid."

Noah bites his bottom lip. "It's okay to learn from this but take it from someone who knows. Don't dwell. Don't let it eat you alive from the inside out. It's not worth it."

"Thanks, Noah," I say. "But I think I just need some time to process everything." I turn to leave, but he grabs my arm.

"Come on," he says. "Don't be like that, Matt..." He freezes, but it's too late. He's just called me by his dead ex's name. "I-I d-didn't mean..."

"Whatever," I say, trying not to feel hurt but feeling it

all the same. It's as if I asked the universe if I could feel any worse and the universe answered *yes*. "Let's just get out of here." I head to the others who are crouched down by the closed door of the room. I crouch down beside them, as does Noah behind me.

"There's a room across the hall from this one," says Dawson. "A big one, which curves around to a door to the next hallway over. From there we should be able to make it to the elevators. They should be running on the backup generator. They'll be slow, but they'll get us where we need to go. One of them goes straight up to my office where there's a remote station which is voice activated. It should still be running despite the outage. I should be able to manually bring the entire park back online. At that point, defenses should kick in and help us out. Then we can radio the mainland and get everyone out of here."

"Everyone?" I ask.

"All of us as well as the rest of the park guests," he says.

"We didn't see anyone outside," says Mr. Zeckel.

"Of course you didn't," says Dawson. "Emergency protocol has park security pull all guests into underground bunkers until they get the all clear. There's a whole labyrinth of tunnels under the park, just like Disney World. The only difference is that we never made that information public."

"Everyone's alive?" I ask, thrilled at this shred of good news.

"I don't know about everyone. But anyone that was within the perimeter of Town Square or one of the resorts when the power went down should be. We take safety very seriously here."

"Obviously," says Zach sarcastically.

"How do we get to the room across the hall with those things out there?" asks Janice, for once bringing the rest of us back on track. She looks terrible. Her makeup has streaked down her face and she's wrapped her arms around herself, trying to stop from shivering. But now that I think about it, I'm pretty cold too. My best guess is that the frigid air is related to the wendigos, who are partial to a cool climate and whose breath can literally turn things to ice.

"Quietly," is Dawson's answer. I peer up at the windows of our room, only now realizing that they aren't foggy from age or not having been cleaned. They're not foggy at all. They're frosted over, covered in what I now see is a glimmering coat of ice.

Dawson pulls down on the door's handle and then pushes it open enough to peak out. "Single file. Move slowly. If we rush, we're dead. If we make any noise, we're dead."

"Think you could tone it down on the 'death' stuff for the kids?" asks Mr. Zeckel.

"No," says Dawson with an angry glare. Mr. Zeckel looks a little embarrassed. He's not usually on the receiving end of discipline.

Dawson pushes the door open a little more and squeezes through. Staying crouched, he moves across the hall, opens the door to the opposite room and squeezes inside. Then he turns and beckons whoever dares to go next. To my surprise, shivering Erika, moves next. She's silent as she crosses the hallway. She and Dawson disappear, hiding behind the wall in the opposite room. Janice follows, quiet as a mouse. Thomas goes next. He's quiet until he reaches the opposite door. He barely nudges it as he squeezes through, but it's enough to send a harsh creaking echo down the hall.

The wendigo turns at the end of the hallway and we all recoil into our rooms. I sit closest to our door, which is still ajar, and in the reflection of its metal doorknob, I can see the beast stomping its hooved feet down the hall towards us. It notices our door open. And though these animals are in no way intelligent, I can see the confusion on its bloody face. It knows something is amiss. It takes in a breath, its exposed chest muscles and bones expanding, then huffs the breath out, causing a cloud of icy mist to form and drift in front of it.

The wendigo approaches us. It reaches out its clawed hand and places it on the door. I see its hand in the flesh rather than in a reflection. I retreat against the wall, hoping it won't see me in the reflection now that it's so close. My breath is heavy as I try to remain calm. I can hear Mr. Zeckel, Noah and Zach next to me, also trying not to freak out. Any moment, this creature is going to come into the room and then we'll be totally screwed. Totally trapped.

There's a very audible clattering noise from down the hallway, back in the direction the wendigo just came from. Someone is trying to distract the beast. It turns its head with its hand still on the door, contemplating what is more pressing to investigate. Finally, it turns away and heads back down the hall. I don't waste this moment. I dash across the hallway into the opposite room, passing right behind the wendigo. I come into the room quickly and quietly and sit, placing my back against the wall. Thomas sits right beside me with the others next to him. Our heads are all lined up, directly beneath a window.

The room is surprisingly long, lined with several cubicles directly in front of us. To my right, past Dawson on the end, I can see where the room curves to the right, out of sight.

Suddenly, a loud thump reverberates up from the floor.

Don't look up, I tell myself. Another thump. *Do not look up.* Each one gets a little closer. Thump. *Don't you dare.* Each one a little louder. THUMP! I look up as the wendigo's paw comes through the glass, shattering the window into a million pieces which rain down on us.

Janice and Erika let out small, stifled gasps. We all cower and shield our heads instinctively. Thomas' breath quivers next to me. I try simply to hold my breath, scared to make any sound. In hindsight, coming across the hallway to this room now seems like the worst choice I could have made. I yearn to go back to the other side. Back to safety. My eyes wander up as the wendigo's head enters through the window. At any moment, it could look down and there we would be. It inhales sharply. When it exhales, a cloud of white mist blows out from its nostrils and then, like gently falling snow, descends, landing atop Thomas's head. I watch as his hair turns to solid ice, the brown color draining from it, replaced by a stark white.

He stares at me, his eyes wide with terror. I can see ice crystals forming and slowly snaking down the skin of his forehead. I shake my head, trying to soundlessly convince him to stay quiet. He's panicking. I can see it in his eyes. His head shakes from side to side as a single tear falls from his right eye and freezes on his cheek. Above us, the wendigo pulls its head back out of the window.

Thomas screams, raking his hands through his hair, breaking up the ice and pulling the rest of it from his scalp. White shards of ice fall to the floor and shatter. The wendigo does not grace us with its head this time. It reaches through the wall, grabs Thomas by his chest and rips him out of the room.

"Fuck!" I hear Dawson yell from the other side of Erika and Janice. He waves the two girls to follow him, but they're both freaking out. I stand up to see that the wendigo has thrown Thomas into the opposite wall in the hall. He slumps on the floor beneath a Thomas-sized dent. The wendigo moves in on him, but Mr. Zeckel jumps out of the room across the hall and aims his trusty flare gun at the beast. The flare gun fires, blinding all of us momentarily as the wendigo erupts into flames and disintegrates to dust. An ice-based creature susceptible to fire isn't the most original thing Mythos has ever thought up, but right now I'm happy for it.

"Go!" says Mr. Zeckel, shoving Noah and Zach towards us. He reaches down and grabs Thomas, standing him upright and pushing him forward, before quickly reloading the flare gun with one of the remaining flares on the clip. All four of them dash into the room and we all head down the row of cubicles filled with old computer monitors, dusty books and rolling chairs. The path veers right, leading us into an adjoining room, which is connected to a new hallway parallel to the one we just left. Dawson, in the lead, throws a door open and we all pile through. At the end of the hall, I can see two elevators. This hallway is just as dimly lit as the last, but at least there are no wendigos in it. Of course, just the thought of our good fortune jinxes our luck.

Behind us, there's a crash as three wendigos explode through the wall from the room we just emerged out of. I guess when a creature is that strong, they don't need to worry about learning to use door handles.

"Run!" yells Zach, but it's entirely unnecessary. Who wouldn't run with these terrible creatures chasing after them? Two wendigos down the hall lunge onto the walls on either side of us and begin crawling along them like hellish spiders. The third inhales deeply, then breathes out a thick cloud of icy mist on the floor. The cement isn't only covered in ice, it transforms into it instantaneously. The ice spreads out along the floor, right under Mr. Zeckel who has fallen to the back. It takes hold of his foot, climbing up his ankle and turning his lower leg to ice, forcing him to lose his balance and fall. This all happens fast yet I see it as if in slow motion. He reacts to the fall, reaching out his arms to catch the ground, and in doing so, loses control of the flare gun, tossing it to me. TO ME! *Mr. Can't Catch.* Mr. Zeckel has just signed his own death certificate.

No. I can do this. I *have* to do this. Now is the one time in my life where I have to get this right. I lock my eyes on the gun as it arcs through the air. I reach out. I'm going to do it. I'm actually going to catch something. The wendigos round on Mr. Zeckel, coming at him as he lies helplessly frozen to the ground. The ice is all the way up to his knee on the one leg now. I open my palms and then . . . the gun bounces off my fingertips and topples past me through the air.

I missed it. I fucking missed it.

But as I turn, I see Janice grab the gun out of the air, already aiming it down the hallway. "Get down!" she yells. I duck as she fires off the gun, plugging all three of the wendigos, one at a time, reloading between each one, like a badass terminator! The succession of each blast of light leaves Mr. Zeckel squirming on the ground.

"Holy shit, Janice," I say. And then, just so I never sound cool ever, I add: "You did a thing!"

She shrugs. "I think guns are lame, but Daddy insists on taking me to the gun range. He says if I'm going to be so pretty, I need to be able to defend myself against bad men." She raises her eyebrows at the dust which was once the wendigos. "Ugly, hairy, deer men." She pulls the gun's barrel in front of her face and blows the smoke off of it. I honestly think it's the most badass thing I've ever seen in real life.

Noah and Zach run past me and help Mr. Zeckel to his feet. In the commotion, his frozen leg has shattered just above the knee, leaving him with only one working leg. For the rest of his life, Mr. Zeckel will only have one leg. The gravity of that sinks in as well as the realization that if not for Janice, he could have lost a hell of a lot more. He could be dead. And that would have been my fault. I can't help but wonder if a day will ever come where I stop feeling like such a failure.

Zach and Noah pull Mr. Zeckel's arms over their shoulders and help him down the hall. We all convene in front of the two elevators. Mr. Zeckel is essentially out of commission and Thomas is still scratching at his hair, freaking out.

"I'm s-sorry I s-screamed," he sputters. "It was just so cold. So cold it felt hot. Like my scalp was burning. I still feel it." He breaks down and sobs. He looks as though the experience has traumatized him. And who knows if his hair will ever stop being blindingly white.

"Everyone ready?" asks Dawson, placing his hand on

a digital screen next to the elevator to our right. The doors slowly open. I look around at everyone. I don't think they're ready at all.

"Look," says Zach. "I know splitting up might sound like a terrible idea, but let's get real. Mr. Zeckel can't take any more action. Neither can Thomas. We need to get them somewhere safe." We all glance around at each other.

"Well you're coming with me," says Dawson, staring at me. "Turning on the power essentially paints a target on us, and I'd like to have the kid who thinks he can beat the vampire by me when that happens."

"I'll stay with Mr. Zeckel and Thomas," says Zach.

"Me too," says Janice. "No offense, but I already did my part." Apparently, Janice has fulfilled her helpfulness quota for the day.

"You have to stay with them too," I say to Noah.

"No," he says angrily. "I'm not going to let you go off with this asshole and get yourself killed." Dawson rolls his eyes.

"Gee, thanks," he says.

"You have to," I say. "Zach can't carry Mr. Zeckel by himself. They need you. I can do this."

Noah stares me in the eyes, and I don't look away, which feels weird and scary and right all at the same time. "Okay," says Noah. "But before you go," he leans in. I'm guessing he means to kiss me, but I hold my hands to his chest and stop him.

"Stop," I say.

"Oh," he says, deflated. "I'm sorry, I just thought—"

"If I kiss you now, I'll always have to remember my first kiss being in a dark hallway that smells like a funeral home. First kisses should be magical. Mine included." He pulls away. "Save it for me, okay?"

There's some serious tension between me and Noah. And sure, he has some intense baggage from his ex. But I *do* want to kiss him. I know that's probably just my desperation playing tricks with my mind again, but I do. Just not here. Not now. Noah respectfully pulls away.

"Get them out of here," I say. "Please." I look at Janice and Erika.

Janice is focused on helping Thomas pull ice out of his hair. Erika looks me squarely in the eyes. She comes straight up to me and holds me in her arms. "Guessing I can't come with you?"

"Not a chance," I say. "I need you to get to safety. You're my best friend. And besides, I'm sort of the man in our relationship. I should really be the one running into danger."

She steps back, still holding both my hands, and squints. "Are you though?"

"Are you saying I'm not?"

"You do make me kill a lot of spiders."

"One time."

"And open jars for you."

"I can't open jars," says Thomas out of nowhere. "I've got weak joints in my arms."

"We know!" says everyone at once.

Erika brings her attention back to me and hugs me again. "Be safe."

"You too," I say, hugging her back.

"I love you Henry."

"I love you too, Beyoncé." She pulls back, wiping a few tears from her eyes as she laughs.

Dawson opens the left elevator, and everyone piles in except for the two of us. We all wave as the elevator door closes. And then they're gone.

"Alright kid," says Dawson as we step into the right elevator. "You ready to save Mythos?" The doors close. I can remember a time when all I ever wanted was to meet Dawson Saks. Now I find myself wanting more than anything to get this all over with so that I never have to see him again.

"Yeah," I say. But as I stand in the elevator, watching the numbered lights flicker on and off in ascending order, I can't help but wonder if Mythos, this place that I've fantasized about, this place that I've obsessed over, deserves to be saved.

SEVENTEEN

The elevator comes to a groaning stop and the doors slide open. I've seen Dawson Saks' office before in Vincent's memories, but now that I'm here, it looks even larger and grander than before. Unbelievably high ceilings hang over sparse but exquisite furniture, and a wall-to-wall, floor-to-ceiling window looks out over the entire park. It's dusk now and the sun hasn't quite settled down for the night, casting gentle hues of purple and pink in the sky. But I don't have any time to bask in any of this, because the office is not, as we expected, empty.

Vincent stands in the center of the room, staring out the window with his back to us. He's surrounded by grey statues which weren't here in the memory. They resemble soldiers all holding rifles aimed at Vincent. But the more I look at them, the more I realize they aren't statues at all. Or at least they didn't start out that way. These unmoving soldiers were once actual soldiers, presumably ones that came here to stop Vincent, just like we're here to do. Somehow, he's turned them to stone.

"I'm gaining new powers every day," says Vincent, continuing to stare out the window. "Take these men for example. I didn't know I could turn them to stone until I did it." Now he turns and looks right at us. "Now they're sort of like your little amusement park, Dawson."

Dawson is not one bit amused by the sight of his soldiers being murdered. I recognize one of the soldiers as the man from Vincent's memories. Richard, I think his name was. His expression is frozen with his mouth open. I imagine the word 'Fire!' bursting from his lips. Turns out, it was his last.

"Solid as stone, but so easily broken." He holds up his hand and snaps his fingers. All the statues break apart and crumble to the ground into piles of grey dust, no longer resembling the people they once were.

This ends now. I came here with a purpose. Vincent's reign of terror is over. If I can believe a lock into opening or a unicorn into healing, then I can do this too. I think about how vampires were never a part of Mythos. I tell myself the only reason I think Vincent is a vampire at all is because Dawson said so. But is he really? After all, he doesn't have any fangs. He doesn't drink blood, at least that I've seen. He doesn't sleep in a coffin or turn into a bat. Which can only mean one thing.

"Vincent," I say, stepping forward, trying to muster

as much bravery as I've got left in me.

"Yes, my prince?" he says sweetly.

It's now or never. "Dawson tried to create a vampire. But you aren't one. Dawson failed. You don't exist!"

I wait for him to vanish or burst into dust or explode into light. Any of the things that should happen right when you trick the final boss if my sources—Hollywood movies—are correct. But none of them do. Nothing happens at all. Nothing. He just stands there as a sly smile creeps across his face.

Sweat beads on my forehead. It's not working. "I . . . I don't believe in you!"

"Oh Henry," he says. "Did you really think you could just not believe in me and I'd go away? I'm standing right in front of you. You can't just not believe what's right in front of your eyes."

"He's right," says Dawson in a whisper. "The human brain doesn't work that way. Sight is the most powerful purveyor of belief. Seeing is believing."

"Besides, I'm practically a part of you now. You can't just forget about me." Vincent chuckles.

"What are you talking about?" I ask.

"Didn't you notice me there in the back of your thoughts?"

I suddenly replay every moment over the past two

days where I felt as though Vincent was there, watching me, judging me. And now, coupled with the fact that I know what he really is, I finally understand why. "You glamoured me!?"

"Like I said, I'm gaining new powers every day."

Dawson turns to me. "Happen to have a Plan B?"

My heart is pounding. My stomach feels as though it's just flipped over on itself. This was my big plan. My *only* plan. This was my chance to get it right and redeem myself. And I failed. I turn to Dawson and shake my head.

"Alright then," he says. He looks up at Vincent. "Computer. Bring all park systems back online."

"Password please," says a female voice above us.

Dawson's voice catches in his throat. "Patricia."

"Password accepted." The lights in the room burst to life. Outside, we watch as blinking lights begin to pop up all over the park. Electrical fences come back online. Security systems flicker to life once more. Below us, in the distance, I can hear the music in Town Square begin to play.

"Anomaly detected," says the female voice. "Subject identified as Vampire is outside designated parameters. Emergency protocols initiated."

Vincent smiles as ten panels disappear from the ceiling above him, replaced by large guns which lower into the room. The guns all aim at Vincent and then shoot out long streams of fire. The heat washes over us in waves, causing me to recoil as the flames envelop Vincent. But he doesn't burn. His body heals itself as the fire hits him. He reaches his hands up, palms open, then closes his hands into fists. The guns crumple in on themselves and then fall from the ceiling, crashing into the floor with several heavy thuds, leaving the last of the fire to dissipate into thin air.

Dawson yells, completely losing his composure. This is not the Dawson Saks I've always known from television. He charges at Vincent and wraps his hands around the vampire's neck. He uses all his strength to choke Vincent, but Vincent simply smiles.

"Powerless," says Vincent. "Just like the creatures you've shoved into cages and tortured for so many years. Vincent grabs Dawson's throat with his right hand, easily lifting him into the air. Unlike Vincent, Dawson immediately begins to gasp for breath, releasing his hands from Vincent's neck and grabbing at the hand now around his own, desperately trying to free himself. "Your reign over Mythos is ended," says Vincent. He spins around and hurls Dawson's body towards the window.

"No!" I yell. But my words are useless. Dawson's body flies through the window, shattering the entire wall. He falls out of sight along with all the glass, leaving the window open to the park beyond. A cool summer breeze spills into the room. Vincent turns back to me.

"At last," he says. "It's just you and me."

"It will never be just you and me," I say, rage building in my chest. "Not now. Not ever. I am not going to be your prince. I am not going to watch you destroy everything and everyone I love. I didn't see it at the start, but I see it now. You are pure evil."

A crushing pain fills my head and Vincent's eyes bare down on me, getting inside my mind. As he speaks, I don't so much hear his words as feel them coursing through my veins. I'm completely at his mercy.

"I am what that man made me!" yells Vincent, no longer looking at me with kind eyes.

"You got a shitty deal," I confess, forcing my eyes to focus on him despite the throbbing pain behind them. "You did. I saw it. But lots of people get shitty deals. Lots of people are born to families that suck or lose people they love or don't get what they want. But that does not mean they get a free pass to burn the world down around them. You had a choice. We all have a choice. The moment you escaped this place, you had the choice to walk away. Hell, with your abilities, you could've made the world a *better* place. You could've taken the shitty hand you were dealt and turned it into something truly great. You *had* a choice, and you chose pain and death."

"I chose to do to them exactly what they did to me," he says. "They let me burn to death so many times. They chose to make an enemy of me. And now I'm offering you the same choice. You can help me finish what I started, or you can die here, Henry."

I feel his voice echoing through my bones, through every muscle of my body, trying to convince me to just give up and say yes. Through gritted teeth I manage to push back. "I'd rather die." I don't want to, but I also have no intention of watching this creature I've helped unleash destroy more lives.

"Wrong choice, Henry," he says. He holds up his hand and fires a bolt of grey electricity at me. I close my eyes and wait for the end to come.

"No!" A voice erupts from behind me. I'm shoved aside, and I topple helplessly to the floor. I scramble to position myself to see who else is here.

Noah. My eyes land on him, turned to stone by the door.

A noise pours out of me like it's coming from every inch of my being. A sound I've never heard myself make before. So primal. With all the pain of losing Noah. My heart breaks. My mind breaks. Somehow, I make my way to Noah. I place my shaking hands on his stony face. His green eyes have been replaced by grey rock. "No, no, no!" I can't bear this. Tears pour down my face.

A weight on my mind I didn't even realize was there suddenly shatters. Vincent's glamour has lifted. Everything is suddenly so crisp and clear. I'm not the reason all of this is happening. Vincent is. Dawson is. I'm not a terrible person. They are. All along, Vincent's influence nudged me to indulge my doubt and blame myself for everything so that when the time came, I'd feel so sorry for myself that I'd roll over and give in to him. But I'm stronger than that. I'm better than that. Noah's right. I'm a good person, or at least I try to be, and in this world, that means something.

"Humans are so fragile," says Vincent from behind me. "It never ceases to amaze me." I turn to look at him. He raises a hand up in front of his face. "They always break."

He barely finishes his words as I charge into him, faster than I've ever moved before. Even though I've managed to surprise him, he's still much stronger than me. He grabs me by my shirt and throws me over his head. I slam face first into the floor, facing the window. Vincent looms over me at my feet.

"Give up, Henry!" He slowly turns his back on me. "Why keep fighting? From the moment I first woke up in that tank, no one has ever been able to kill me. Do you honestly believe you can? Do you honestly think that desperate, whiny Henry is the answer? You're alone. You've always been alone. You can't save anyone, and no one is coming to save you, so just give up!"

As I turn onto my back, I catch a glimpse of a silhouette in the distance. A shape that only two days earlier would have struck fear into my heart. Its majestic wings flap as it comes into focus, getting nearer by the second. If not for my help, that dragon might be dead by now. I did that. I saved that beautiful creature. I'm not useless. I'm capable of doing something good for someone else. But what does that mean? Do I honestly think that just because I can do good that I can actually defeat Vincent?

I don't know. What I believe has changed so much in the last couple of days. What I think of as true has shifted dramatically. And a big part of that is Noah. He believed that there was good in the world. But not just in the world, in *me* too. It's amazing how other people can see something in you that you could never see in yourself. It's amazing how crushingly hard we can be on ourselves.

As the creature gets closer, I push myself up from the floor. Vincent moves towards the center of the room and turns back around, rolling his eyes at my continued efforts.

"I believe a lot of things," I say, looking off to the

distant horizon. My chest hurts to speak. Chances are good that I broke a rib when I slammed into the floor. "I believe that cookies are, hands down, the best food that has ever been invented." I allow a small smile to part my lips. "I believe people are more than just one thing." Noah taught me that. People aren't good or evil or happy or sad. They're a million different things all at once, and those million different things change by the second. "I believe that there is good in the world." He taught me that too. "I believe that unicorns can heal." I've believed that since the first time I ever saw one drawn on a page in that book that my grandma used to read to me. *My Friend, The Unicorn.* That book probably started my crazy obsession with Mythos. It was a book about the unicorn and all his friends and as I stand here now, I remember each of them in turn. A unicorn which healed the sick, a fairy which granted its friends the ability to fly, and a dragon which breathed the most amazing blue fire.

I turn to Vincent. "I may not be perfect, but thanks to that guy right there," I look to Noah's stone body, "I've realized something very important about myself. It's not that I don't believe that you're a vampire, or that you don't exist. It's that I don't believe in you! What you stand for. How you see the world." I place my hand on my chest. "But I do believe in me." That's not something I've ever said out loud before, which I realize now is a total shame because saying it feels so friggin' amazing. I sigh as the sound of the dragon's wings beat in my ears. "And most importantly, I believe that dragons can breathe fire."

The smile on Vincent's face vanishes as the green dragon lands on the exposed ledge, just inside the shattered window beside me.

"No," says Vincent beginning to feign a laugh. But I can hear the trembling fear in his voice. "They don't!"

"Yes," I say. "They do." A soft glow begins in the dragon's throat and works its way up the creature's long neck until, at last, a stream of blue flame explodes from the dragon's mouth, washing over Vincent and disintegrating him to dust until nothing is left.

The dragon coughs out one last ember of flame, turns, and flaps its large leathery wings, taking off into the sky again.

I run to Noah and place my hands on his stone-cold chest. Tears begin to roll down my cheeks. I shake my head in disbelief.

"Why? Why did you come back?" He doesn't respond. He can't. I turn to look out over the park and think about our journey over the last several days. How far we've come. How much we've survived. All the creatures we once thought to be only fairy tales. This place is the result of dreams made real. Not just dreams, but childhood fantasies too. This is the creation of a man who wanted so much to live in a world where anything you could imagine, anything you could believe, could be real.

Fairy tales taught me plenty as a child. I imagine they taught a lot of people a lot of things. They taught me to whistle while I work and wish on shooting stars. They taught me to believe that dreams can come true. They taught me about princesses and princes, and they taught me that magic can come from the smallest places—from a bed knob, to a lamp, to a lost slipper . . . or even a kiss.

I turn back to Noah. It's absurd, but I've always believed that my first kiss would be magical. I've believed it since I was a little kid. Even when it turned out that Santa and the Easter Bunny weren't real, I still held onto this. I walk up to him, hold his cold face in my hands and place my lips on his. For a moment, everything is still, and then slowly, warmth returns to his face.

I pull back and look right into Noah's emerald green eyes. I smile and cry at the same time.

"Henry," he says. "Why are you crying?"

"Because," I say. "You're alive."

"Of course, I am," he says. "What else would I be?"

"I-I saved you," I choke on my words.

"It's about time."

We kiss again and as long as I've been waiting for this moment, I can't help but think that it's nothing like what I imagined or believed it would be. It's so much more.

.

EPILOGUE

Back outside in the Town Square, we find that people have emerged from the underground bunkers and are now being led to the ships that will take us all away from the island. Night has fallen, but harsh lights from the street and emergency vehicles illuminate the aftermath of the fall of Mythos. As we move through the crowd, two paramedics carrying a stretcher walk by, and a hand reaches out to me, grabbing my arm.

"Henry!" I look down to see Dawson Saks laying on the stretcher. "You're alive. That means . . ."

"Vincent's gone," I say.

"But . . . how?"

I kneel down and stare into the eyes of the man who was once my hero. "Why, magic of course. What else?" These were the words he always parroted whenever asked how he was able to create the creatures of Mythos.

"No," says Dawson as the paramedics carry him away. "You have to tell me! HENRY!" I let him fade into the crowd. I notice Zach and Janice before they notice me.

Shocker of the century, they're fighting.

"I'm sorry Janice. I just can't do this. I can't lie to myself anymore," says Zach.

"Lie to yourself?" asks Janice. "What, are you gay now?"

"No!"

"Whatever," she says. "I'm going to go hit up Thomas. His white hair is super-hot." She turns, tosses her hair, which has somehow managed to stay looking flawless throughout this entire debacle, and storms off.

Zach sighs and then turns to walk towards Erika, who I now notice is helping Mr. Zeckel onto a stretcher of his own. His missing leg looks way worse out here under the harsh lights. Zach waits for Mr. Zeckel to be secured before he taps Erika on the shoulder. She turns to him, startled.

"Oh, hey Zach," she says.

"Hey, Erika." He gulps. "Listen. What Henry said about lying to himself. I think I've been doing that too. I, uh, well what I mean to say is . . ."

Erika grins at him and raises an eyebrow.

"I . . . um . . . for a while actually, I've, uh, liked you?" He half-heartedly confesses.

"Is that a question?" she asks, teasing him.

"No," says Zach, turning red. "What I mean to say is

that . . . I like you."

Erika smiles and shakes her head. "Took you long enough." She stands on her toes and kisses him on the cheek. It's not the kind of kiss that would bring someone back from the dead, but it's still sweet and I'm sure the first of many more to come.

"Cool," says Zach.

"Ugh," she groans, playfully pushing him away. She turns and that's when she sees me. "Henry!" she runs up and wraps her arms around me. Zach joins her and so does Noah and we all just hold each other in this big group hug.

"So, is it over?" asks Erika as we pull apart.

"It's over," I say.

Her eyes dart between Noah and me. "And you guys . . ."

Neither of us says anything.

"Well Zach and I were just going to see if anyone needs any help. We'll uh, leave you guys to talk?" Erika gives my arm one more squeeze, then grabs Zach's hand and leads him into the crowd.

Noah and I don't talk at first. We just walk off into a small clearing, away from the everyone else. "Look," I finally say. "I can't just be some replacement for your . . . for Matthew."

297

"I know," he says.

"And I can't just jump into something again, like I did with Vincent."

"I'm not a vampire."

"I know that, but," I sigh. "I know so little about you."

"So, what do we do?" he asks.

I think about it for a long moment. "What if we start fresh?"

"What do you mean?"

I step back and extend my hand. "Hey, you're new at school this year, right?" I say casually. "I'm Henry. I think we have Calc together?"

He grins and takes my hand. We shake. "Noah," he says. "Nice to meet you."

"So," I say shyly, still shaking his hand. I look him in the eyes, and maybe for the first time in my life, eye contact doesn't make me feel like a wreck. "I really like your eyes."

"Thanks," he says. "I got them at Target. One of their black Friday deals." We laugh.

"Would you, want to grab a coffee sometime?" I ask. "I just had this crazy vacation at Mythos, and I'm dying to talk to someone about it."

"That's so crazy, I was just at Mythos too!"

"Get out!" I say, overdramatically.

He grins, and I realize that his gorgeous eyes only become more gorgeous when he smiles. "I'd love to, but I don't drink coffee," he says, swaying side-to-side sheepishly, grabbing hold of both my hands. "I'd much rather grab a cookie."

"Wow," I say turning red. "That is the most beautiful thing anyone has ever said to me."

As the days go by, we'll learn about all the lives that were lost on Mythos. We'll be interviewed and questioned so many times that we'll feel like robots as we repeat the same answers over and over again. We'll learn that Dawson Saks lost his ability to walk after the fall. We'll learn that most of the people in the runaway tram didn't survive. Mythos will be closed permanently as the mounting pile of lawsuits against the park grows by the day. Animal rights activists and governments all over the world will launch into an epic ethical and legal debate about the now free-roaming animals on the island. None of the animals make any attempt to leave their home, but who knows if or when that will change. The park may be closed but for the foreseeable future, all eyes are still on Mythos.

As for Noah and me, it's anyone's guess as to what comes next. But I'm excited to get to know him. I'm excited to build something with him that's more than just a crush or a desire to be liked by someone, anyone, else. I'm excited to learn his favorite food and his favorite book and his favorite everything. And though I can't be sure what the future will bring for us, I believe our greatest adventure is yet to come.

ACKNOWLEDGEMENTS

I often wish that the ideas in my head could magically birth onto the page simply by me believing in them enough. Sadly, real life isn't quite as incredible as the island of Mythos. Writing is a labor of love, patience, time and dedication. Mythos is the most personal thing I've ever written. Sure, on the surface it's a fantastical story, but the characters found here live because of many of my own personal anxieties, struggles and worries. As you can imagine, this made writing it down feel like an emotional roller-coaster. Luckily, I had some pretty amazing people to help me along the way.

First off, I want to give a huge thank you to LaQuita Brown, for whom this book is dedicated. Mythos was originally written as part of the NaNoWriMo challenge. For those who don't know, that means writing the first draft of a novel in 30 days or less. LaQuita, who also took the challenge, acted as a cheerleader for me, reading pages and encouraging me to keep going. Without her, I can guarantee this book would not have seen the light of day.

I also want to thank Jonathan and James for beta reading this book in its earliest form and giving me some really amazing feedback and suggestions. It can be very scary to give a first draft to new readers, but these guys were amazing and kind, and ultimately helped this book click in ways I hadn't even considered. Thanks you two!

I have to give a huge shout out to Jonathan Perry, the illustrator for Mythos' cover. Not only did he create a cover which encapsulates this story perfectly, he made the whole process easy and fun. And even when I thought I was sending him a million notes at once, he always took everything to heart and put me at ease with one simple word: "Rad."

As always, I have to thank my Mom and Grandma who always support my efforts to tell crazy stories like this one. In many ways, my Mom is to blame for *Mythos*. The first book I really remember her reading me before bed was *Jurassic Park*, and I think my love for that story shows throughout this book. My mom raised me as a single parent, so just the fact that she found time to read me a Michael Crichton novel after her long work shifts deserves applause and my eternal gratitude.

Of course, none of this is possible without my husband, Carl Li, who not only helped to edit this book, giving up many MANY hours of his life, but also put up with my stress and anxiety as I worked to pull this book together. His support and love are constants in my life, and he always perfectly balances encouragement with critique. He also knows when cookies are needed. Spoiler: Cookies are ALWAYS needed.

And finally, thank you for taking the time to read this story which has, in many ways, lived with me all my life. So many ideas I've had for so many years have finally found life in this book and I'm thrilled to be able to share them with you, at long last. I hope it reminds you that the most magical moment in any day is one where we remember to believe in ourselves. I also hope it encourages you to eat more cookies.

-Jaysen Headley

ABOUT THE AUTHOR

Jaysen Headley was born and raised in Lakewood, Colorado. Eventually, he packed up and headed to New York City where he met his husband, and editor, Carl Li. They now live in Orlando, Florida, with their dog Izzy, where they go to theme parks, eat delicious treats and have tons of fun every day.

Jaysen loves to read books, play board games and blast away at monsters in a good video game. He is also an avid healthy eater unless it comes to cookies. He will forego any diet in the name of a good cookie!

Jaysen is also the author of *A Love Story for Witches, A Home for Wizards* and *Longtails: The Storms of Spring*, all of which can be found in store and on Amazon and Kindle.

Also Available

A Love Story for Witches

Available in Print and E-book Formats

JaysenHeadleyWrites.com

Longtails

The Storms

Of Spring

Available in Print and E-book Formats

LongtailsSaga.com

Made in the USA
Columbia, SC
07 March 2023

13347889R00186